Sally's
DREAMS

SALLY'S DREAMS

ESTELLE RAUCH

SALLY'S DREAMS

iUniverse books may be ordered through booksellers or by contacting:

iUniverse
1663 Liberty Drive
Bloomington, IN 47403
www.iuniverse.com
1-800-Authors (1-800-288-4677)

*Because of the dynamic nature of the Internet, any web addresses or
links contained in this book may have changed since publication and
may no longer be valid. The views expressed in this work are solely those
of the author and do not necessarily reflect the views of the publisher,
and the publisher hereby disclaims any responsibility for them.*

*Any people depicted in stock imagery provided by Getty Images are
models, and such images are being used for illustrative purposes only.
Certain stock imagery © Getty Images.*

ISBN: 978-1-5320-8551-2 (sc)
ISBN: 978-1-5320-8552-9 (e)

Print information available on the last page.

iUniverse rev. date: 10/14/2019

CHAPTER 1

I t was a gloomy day, cold and windy, a precursor of the snow that would come that night. The Barnard senior, standing on a crowded subway to Penn Station to catch a LIRR train for Thanksgiving weekend at her parents', was forced to backtrack; she had left her overnite bag at the apartment. During her wait for the next train, an amused Sally could imagine mom's over-reaction to the young woman's delay.

Sally's brother, newly returned with his family to Long Island following seven years in Ohio, met her at the Glen Cove LIRR station. To her surprise, he drove them to a park overlooking L.I. Sound. Commenting, "Let's catch up, baby sister," he rejected her response: "Mom will kill us both! And it's freezing." They admired images of haze and clouds touched by hints of sun moving across the winter's sky. A full hour later, he dropped Sally at their parents' home. After exiting his car, supposedly to buy cigarettes, a smiling Sally said, "Mom always let you get away with murder; she'll rip me a new one!"

The family's large Victorian home sits majestically on a hill overlooking Long Island Sound, and seems to the eye, welcoming. The home's front door remains open to receive guests. Duchess, the family's beloved Samoyed, fresh from her own early Thanksgiving feast, flew toward Sally, tail wagging wildly. Hugging her, Sally postponed the inevitable while inhaling delectable odors emanating from the kitchen, and in the long entrance foyer, admired paintings and sculptures that are mother's pride. Hearing a din of familiar voices, she ventured into the great room, while whispering to Duchess, "Mom knows I'm here - but she's punishing me by not leaving her kitchen."

Several of her parents' closest friends stand in front of a warming brick fireplace, devouring hors d'oeuvres and sipping champagne. They greet Sally with words and hugs. The hosts are occupied elsewhere. Mom, busy in the kitchen, finally emerges momentarily to greet her daughter; dad, having stationed himself in his den watching college football with a few of his buddies, barely takes his eyes off the television, nods in response to Sally's greeting. His showing so little interest in her hurts. Most male guests had joined him, though some still wander among the women, unsure where they belong. After their hostess calls guests to table, Rhoda Marcus is observed whispering to her husband, Sam, likely pleading with him to join everyone. Experienced at ignoring her, he responds, "At half-time."

Sam, a short, stocky man meticulously but casually dressed, once seated at the far end of the long bedecked mahogany table concentrates on eating his seafood lasagna, while his son skillfully carves the turkey. Rhoda, opposite Sam and closest to the kitchen, plays her gracious hostess role to perfection, inviting guests to share their holiday preparations. She hopes that others would not notice that their hosts aren't on speaking terms, and that Uncle Bob, morose, possibly drunk, humiliates his well-liked wife, Lily. No one inquires about stunning, absent Aunt Evelyn, who is known to have left husband Ray and their young sons to go off with her lover.

Sally and Aunt Lily, seated far apart, would prefer spending their holidays together at Jazz at Lincoln Center or at the New York City Ballet, but neither would flout Marcus family holiday rules or hurt Rhoda Marcus. Sally had for years wondered why her beloved, popular aunt had married gross Uncle Bob, but lacked the courage to ask her.

Larry proves difficult to engage; after multiple attempts, guests turn to his wife Elisa, who, though pleasant, remains distracted, both by her husband's behavior and by their infant daughter's needs. Twice she excuses herself to take the baby upstairs for nursing and diapering.

Close family friends Anne and Jim and their visiting Italian grandchildren offer a welcome distraction when they begin discussing the upcoming Hanukkah and Christmas holidays. Since they're a 'mixed' couple, he, Catholic, she, Jewish, every year they renegotiate how many outside lights are acceptable, and how big the Christmas tree should be. These are serious decisions for Anne, who even after thirty years is uncomfortable with a dramatic Christmas display. Jim's memories of Christmases in his native Italy allow others to reminisce about their own travels to Italy and what they brought back in the way of leather goods and Venetian glassware. Elisa, raised Catholic, thus far having rejected the notion of converting to Judaism, was silent. Only to herself did she admit that she'd love a Christmas tree; knowing Larry would be disturbed, and heaven knows what her in-laws would think, she had never raised the issue.

Polite but impatient through this conversational blitz, the bored Italian teens and the other young people finally escape to join Uncle Ray's sons at billiards in the home's third floor game room.

Adult guests shift their attention to Sally, who had been relieved at being overlooked. Who is she dating, and what will she be doing after graduation? At last Sam Marcus is interested, and mother Rhoda would be too if she wasn't holed up in her kitchen, where she and the family's housekeeper are busily organizing the dessert presentation. Guests learn that Sally has submitted applications to five law schools, and had taken her L-Sats. An attorney guest whom Sally dislikes lectures her on her choices. She ignores him, rising to help clear the table in preparation for the desserts. Conversation dies. A few women exit to bathrooms while their husbands begin looking at their watches. After sampling the dazzling dessert selection, they express regret at how the horrendous holiday traffic means they must leave. And finally seated for more than a moment, their hostess protests their departure, while Sam can now be the perfect host.

Sally's sister-in-law Elisa had been catapulted into a scene she hadn't anticipated: her in-law's open hostility toward each other, and more disturbing, her husband's withdrawal. Aware of Elisa's pain, Sally whispered, "Larry will be back to normal once he gets away from here. As for our parents..." The younger women hugged Elisa, who, while fighting tears, responded, "I hope so."

An exhausted Rhoda returned to her kitchen, and with the housekeeper's assistance, cleaned up. Sam retreated to his den. Their daughter made her way upstairs, first to gaze at her niece, asleep in a porta-crib in Sally's bedroom.

Hearing her brother and his wife arguing, Sally hesitated momentarily before knocking. From Larry: "You saved my ass, sis. Wifey here was in process of skewering me." And from Elisa: "I'm happy you're here, Sally. We're getting nowhere and we're both exhausted from the duel." Elisa then headed to the bathroom; Sally's arrival had given her an escape.

"I hope you're not about to lecture me too." Larry messed with his sister's hair, adding: "Our darling father was an asshole today comme d'habitude." Sally surprised herself by challenging him. "Yeah, sure. He hates her parties. He resents having to perform - so he doesn't - acts the bad boy part, like a rebellious adolescent."

"Look, I know mom provokes him, always has. If I had married someone like her, I'd have left on our wedding night. Why didn't he? Why did he fuck around instead? Please don't try to tell me that he stayed for us. That's a load of crap."

Sally, grimacing, acknowledged: "I don't know why

5

he stayed. Maybe it wasn't so bad when we were little, or maybe he wanted to save money first, or wait 'til I leave home. I know that mom was complicit with his behavior. She was vigilant, but did she ever suggest counseling?"

"If Elisa and I don't quit this place soon, we're headed for trouble. I stupidly suggested we move to New York after she lost her parents. Then we found out we were expecting. How could I have I believed that our parents would be supportive to Elisa and thrilled with Isabel? You're the only one left, kid, so don't disappear on us." Sally, biting her lower lip, hesitated before responding. "Oh, my god, Larry. If Stanford accepts me, I'm going. Please don't guilt-trip me."

Sally found her father in his office, paying bills. She knew enough not to comment on his recent behavior; he never has tolerated confrontation. Instead, she initiated what she imagined was a neutral subject, Uncle Philip's 'trouble':"It's too bad Uncle Philip and his family couldn't join us today." Getting no response, she took a more direct approach: "Will he have to go to jail?" Dad angrily responded, "You shouldn't assume the worst!"

Sally often wrote in her diary after a stressful family event:

"Leaving dad, I sought out mom to thank her for all the work she had done to make Thanksgiving memorable. Found her in the darkened kitchen. It's always been my favorite room, with spacious windows facing the backyard garden patio, and beyond that, the pool. Tonight the outdoor kitchen was shrouded in gloom, appliances covered, chairs removed to the storage structure. Spring always brings a colorful array of flowering plants, which mom plants under our gardener's scrutiny. But tonight, there were leaves everywhere, practically covering the patio and the pool cover. Why hadn't the place been cleared prior to this holiday?

Seeing my mother so obviously distressed, I touched her hair, and leaning to her level, circled her shoulder, "What's wrong, mom?" Her response shocked me: "Go about your business, Sally. You and your brother have your own agendas. What do you care about me and what I want?"

On the verge of leaving her, I reached for compassion. "Mom, I'm so sorry to have come late. Surely that couldn't have left you so upset."

"Your father is planning something - maybe he's finally gonna leave. Maybe he's found another whore to cheer him up. Nobody's happy around here. So go, Sally. Go!"

Those parent-daughter conversations have me shaken. I must leave New York for law school, even if being so far from everyone I know scares me. Stanford law is a longshot, but if they do accept me, I'm going. Maybe I should apply to UT-Austin as a back-up. Most kids talk to their parents about such a huge decision - but I can't. Dad won't give a damn, and mom will be furious. She feels so unloved. But truthfully, she's been hard to love, always angry. I never know how to comfort her. She doesn't allow herself to be comforted, unless I give in. That can't happen. I promised myself, that wouldn't happen! And now Philip's pressuring me to stay put. How do healthy people choose between what's good for them and what they owe people they love? This time, it has to be about me.

Staring at my image into the hall mirror, I whispered: 'No more home for the holidays for me. That's a promise!'

And that was even before Sally and the world came to learn about how this seemingly innocuous family became notorious.

CHAPTER 2

Barnard had provided a respite from family life from the moment I arrived on campus. A young freshman at sixteen, looking more like thirteen, my fellow out-of-town freshmen still assumed that as a New Yorker, I must be sophisticated. That notion tanked when it became clear that I knew nothing about clubs where 18 year olds could party. Practice with the freshman tennis team and the challenge of a heavy credit load helped support my claim to mother and to my high school boyfriend that I couldn't possibly go home on weekends.

These years at Barnard, my first sustained venture out of the upper middle-class secular Jewish world of my childhood, introduced me to wealthier and more sophisticated kids here from all over the world. In chem lab I befriended a Pakistani girl from Lahore – she invited me to visit her home - though that never happened - and found what I hope will be a lifelong friend with a South African gal, Ginger, a cellist who transferred to Juilliard after our freshman year.

Mom has never let up on guilt-tripping me: "My friend Betty's daughter, Dottie, comes home from NYU almost every weekend." Dad, to his credit, never expected that of me: "Enjoy these years, kid. There's nothing like them. Before you know it, they're over, and the work world will engulf you." Thanks, dad! And thanks for paying the $70,000 annual ticket.

My parents had come together around my applying to law schools. Dad was pushing Harvard or Yale; mom thought my attending Columbia or NYU would be perfect. Both were shocked when I elected to apply to Stanford, a long shot, so they didn't take it seriously.

If Stanford accepts me, I won't be here for Isabel's first steps or to hear her first words. How can I hold onto the special bond I've developed with Elisa? And I will miss the regular trips to theatre and museums with Aunt Lily. Several of my New York friends are already scattered everywhere, including a brilliant guy friend leaving for graduate work in international economics and political science at LSE.

I have had a disturbing habit of walking away from friendships, so there is not one friend I'll miss terribly. Here my parents are blameless. They both have friends from early childhood and each is close to a sibling. In my case, from one year to another, I dropped girl friends. I do remember a disturbing conversation on the subject where my supposedly best high school friend, Catherine, challenged me after I told her, "People can be replaced." An apparently shocked Catherine responded, "You can't be serious, Sally. How can you really care for somebody, have them love you, without feeling devastated when it's over. And not by your choice?"

I didn't say a word. So she continued: "I can't believe you're so cold. It's healthy to care. Like, if you stopped being my best friend, I'd feel awful." So I showed her.

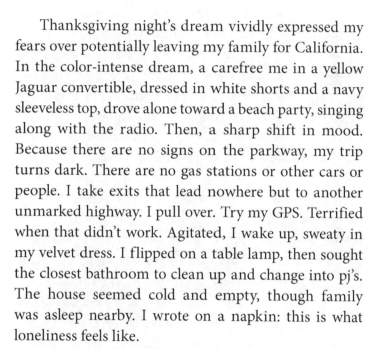

Thanksgiving night's dream vividly expressed my fears over potentially leaving my family for California. In the color-intense dream, a carefree me in a yellow Jaguar convertible, dressed in white shorts and a navy sleeveless top, drove alone toward a beach party, singing along with the radio. Then, a sharp shift in mood. Because there are no signs on the parkway, my trip turns dark. There are no gas stations or other cars or people. I take exits that lead nowhere but to another unmarked highway. I pull over. Try my GPS. Terrified when that didn't work. Agitated, I wake up, sweaty in my velvet dress. I flipped on a table lamp, then sought the closest bathroom to clean up and change into pj's. The house seemed cold and empty, though family was asleep nearby. I wrote on a napkin: this is what loneliness feels like.

Will I be able to make the kinds of friends in the future who I can hold onto? That means dealing with my fluctuating self-image which has left me wrecking or abandoning friends who I feel are in some way, superior to me. I added to my note: CHANGE!

The day after Thanksgiving, I found Elisa in the kitchen, nursing Isabel. Larry was out walking Duchess. Neither parent anywhere around. I was startled when, following my telling her about mom's conviction that dad may be leaving her, Elisa strongly disagreed: "You dad is crazy about this baby. He's been wonderful to us, even if Larry can't or won't admit it. I won't just absorb Larry's distrust - his dislike - of his father."

I left Elisa and Isabel, slightly reassured, but not convinced. After all, Elisa is hungry for new parents after her terrible loss, and thus vulnerable to optimistic fantasy. And I know that dad can turn on the charm with beautiful, susceptible women.

Before I left Sea Cliff on Sunday, I witnessed an interesting scene. Larry & dad were watching the Jets game in the den. Isabel, in her mom's arms, reached for dad. He responded, both grandfather and baby giggling with obvious pleasure. A silent Larry stared at this picture, then left the room. Elisa seemed on the verge of following him, likely troubled by her husband's behavior. After a few minutes, hugging everyone, I made my goodbyes. Could Elisa be right about dad?

The Marcus clan will soon get together for my graduation. I will feel sad, but mainly relieved. Dad will be embarrassed by his tears, while mom will proudly exercise her bragging rights, and pretend to love me.

My hope is that Elisa and Larry will forgive me for my decision to leave New York. Since learning of my hoped-for acceptance by Stanford, Larry has kept his distance. That's always been his way. Like our dad, like me. Elisa has not asked about my preparations for leaving. Even when most of our contact was long distance, she had expressed interest in what I was up to. These days, we speak of Isabel, of national and international news, how we both detest everything Trump is perpetrating, and our fears about the mass shootings in our country.

How weird I've been since anticipating leaving New York. For years, I always noticed the unpleasant smells from garbage and street trash, the homeless, intoxicated beggars, the dirty snow in winter. But now I walk around loving everything in sight, the Columbia campus, the rush of students and everyone else on the streets and the packed subways and buses, the elegance of Fifth and Madison Avenues. I didn't even mind the insanity of the Apple Store, where tourists have their pictures taken outside and inside; even with an appointment, getting help requires patience I've never possessed.

After class, a girl I never liked - she also has been on the tennis team and has not exactly been warm to me - suddenly stopped me: "Hey, I heard you got into Stanford Law. I'm headed there too - for psych - we need to keep in touch. Let's exchange cell numbers, okay?" Yeah, okay.

One thing that always bothered me about her, she seemed so sure of herself. Even now: "I've always wanted to be a psychologist. Have you always known you would be a lawyer?" Can I admit even to myself how uncertain I am about everything? Of course I'm not even sure what, as a lawyer, I would want to do. But I hope, pray, that my years at Stanford will fix that.

I babysat twice when Elisa and Larry had to return to Ohio for a wedding, and once to allow them to celebrate their anniversary over a weekend in the Hamptons. Though delighted with my adorable niece and capable from years of babysitting neighbors' kids, spending so much time without adult input left me wondering if I'll ever want to marry and to be a mom. I'm too distractible and much too selfish. Well, this is not the time to worry about that.

And what do I make of my mother's text, just weeks after Thanksgiving:

Don't judge your father too harshly. He was such a young orphan

Ridiculous! She still loves and defends him, no matter what he does to her. I swear, I'll never let a man humiliate me! Why does she? And has she given up the idea of his leaving her? No wonder Larry and I are both nuts, having been raised in this shaky, unpredictable family.

CHAPTER 3

D ad had left his typical message on my cell: "I'm in San Francisco - a business trip. Tonight for dinner? Bring a friend, if you'd like. I'll pick you up at seven." No question about whether it might be inconvenient, if I had to study for a test or write a paper. Sure enough, he came by, enthusiastic about the "...great-looking campus," thrilled that I'm attending such a prestigious law school. We drove into town in his rented Mercedes convertible and spent a cheerful hour sipping frozen strawberry daiquiris at Laurel Court at the Fairmont, where he's staying. He was his buoyant away-from-home self, conversation sprinkled with pride. It's been a great year for business so his sales staff is content and welcoming. They wined and dined him in their homes, where I'm certain he's at his best. Now he's considering purchasing a bigger yacht and is awaiting delivery of a new black Escalade. And he ordered me a Prius, an advance on my birthday. What color did I want? Dad loves delighting people with his generosity.

Leaving the Fairmont, we headed to the Leatherneck, his favorite steak house here. I allowed myself to wonder what he might say if I had suggested we dine at the Thai restaurant at the hotel. Of course he's the tour guide and the one who's paying, and he doesn't welcome input.

When I order roast leg of lamb, he's mildly irritated: "What a rotten choice in the best God-damned steak house on the west coast!" My dinner was excellent, which we knew it would be, fortunate, because it seemed we had run out of conversation. That always made me nervous around him. Would I be one of those people who bores dad? But, no, he's ready with a new subject.

"Listen, kid, it can't be a surprise to you that mom and I are not doing great together. We've decided to take a hiatus. No divorce. Nothing formal. But I'm gonna rent an apartment in Manhattan when I return from Israel. I hope you won't be nasty about it like your brother."

He was right about my not being surprised. I even thought that this decision could explain his elation. But I did have an irresistible urge to violate my own 'never confront dad' policy: "It's about time, dad. I've known my whole childhood about the other women. Who is it now?"

Ignoring my caustic inquiry, dad waved for the check, then drove me back to campus, both of us silent. On arriving he handed me an envelope, accompanied by a sharp "Goodbye kid." In tears, huddled in my down jacket to ward off the outdoor chill, I asked myself, why, after fifteen years of knowing how shaky things have been with my parents, am I devastated? For the moment, aware that I wasn't feeling myself a twenty year-old adult, but a little kid who's been waiting for this news my whole childhood, terrified to add any stress to either parent for fear that'd be the breaking point.

I'd been the quintessential good girl, while Larry had filled the angry boy role til his escape to Oberlin. I was disgusted by my cowardice. Can I change?

As usual, my father had used money to mitigate our conflict: the envelope contained $2500 in cash, a post-dated check for Stanford for next semester, and a card for the dealership where I was to call the guy with my Prius color preference. Given his plan to return to New York for his birthday, why chose to write the check months in advance?

The following morning I overslept, missing my first class. When I later went to my professor's office to explain that I was ill, he urged me to see the campus physician, remarking that I didn't look well.

Within hours I recovered, parental troubles retreating to the safe place I had created for them many years before. But peace is fragile. Exiting my volunteer assignment, I checked my cell phone. My brother had left a cryptic message: "Sally, You had better call mom a-sap. She's in lousy shape. Our wonderful father called her to say he's moving out. Would you believe she's shocked? And how about his delivery? On the phone. That fucking bastard." So mom had been right after all...

My addictions have always worked wonders for me. They are, in order of importance, studying, tennis and a boyfriend. So with first year finals facing me and my four study partners meeting around the clock, my daughterly responsibilities receded after Larry's phone call.

I was certain that dad would not be in touch with me, given our tense interchange, until some time after his return from Israel. During our dinner in San Francisco, he had invited me to La Jolla for a birthday celebration. He planned a year-long rental on the beach, which he assured me I could use with friends. My smart dad didn't seem to get that my tough workload precluded travels to southern California. Knowing from experience that by the time he returned, dad would have forgotten our tiff, I had not worried about the state of our relationship. But May 20th came and went with no word from him, leaving Larry and me more curious than concerned. Then our personal lives intervened.

For me, it was meeting Carlos. A recent Stanford Law graduate working part-time helping first year law students, Carlos is also employed by a small local law firm specializing in criminal law. We had met on campus a few times, with at least a half dozen other students hungry for his input. We gals were more than intellectually smitten with the 6'1" toned, cocoa-complexioned Mexican. He responded to our legal questions with an occasional hint of a smile or grimace, while his dark brown eyes gave the impression that his attention was elsewhere.

I had dated very little since arriving at Stanford, challenged by the workload and by my study group's demand for hours' long meetings. Beyond that, I have never felt particularly confident about my looks, believing I'm too short at 5'3", slim enough at 105 pounds, with my dark brown hair too curly to do much with. I do like my legs, and for a petite girl, have pretty nice breasts. It seemed that my lackluster social life, true of my years at Barnard, would continue at Stanford. A serious relationship had not become a priority until that first encounter with Carlos. So many women were attracted to him - and they were stunning, dressed provocatively, made-up with skill. Inept at flirting, I didn't believe I had a chance. But within a week, some of that $2500 went for a new wardrobe, hairstyle, and a makeup lesson at Saks.

Fate intervened. Arriving at my summer internship, there was Carlos, headed out to interview clients in every jail and prison within a sixty-mile radius. Before leaving, he handed me a paperback novel. (Atwood's "The Handmaid's Tale") I didn't see him again until the following Friday, when he mentioned he was going to a documentary film on racism. I brazenly invited myself along, then rushed to cancel a dinner date with one of my study mates. On the drive over, he complained: "The firm better pay for my gas soon or I'll quit." He doesn't have enough money: "I need to look the part for court, but can't even buy any decent suits."

That first evening together ended abruptly after my suggestion that we go out for a bite after the film, my treat. I waited for over a week, anxiously hoping he would initiate a date. When he didn't, I did. He accepted, laughing at me – "Why should the guy have to take all the risk?" My caustic reply: "I can't imagine that you

19

have many ladies telling you to get lost!" Instead of that crack, I should have asked him why he would imagine I'd refuse him. Is it racial? It was far too early for me to raise the issue. I'm on shaky ground here, never having dated a non-white guy, or a Catholic. Did he know I'm Jewish? Would he care?

No matter my stress over academics, tennis was definite on Fridays. Following my match, Carlos turned up. I was thrilled, knowing it was no accident, but also embarrassed by my sweaty appearance. Meticulous as usual, he ribbed me – did my guy opponent look so wiped out? Afterward, Carlos suggested we go to his pad for me to shower while he'd barbecue burgers and veggies.

He was outside the shower as I exited half-covered by a thin towel. Dinner would wait. The sex I had up until then was a primer. Carlos was patient, clear that I wasn't all that experienced. Afterward, as we lay on his narrow bed, he volunteered that he "had" his first girlfriend when he was twelve, that all Mexican guys consider that a rite of passage. I joked, "Like a Bar Mitzvah?" But when he also said that Mexican girls who expect to be married must be virgins, I asked, "So who do you guys have sex with?" Carlos laughed, said I'm naïve, funny. "Americans are uptight. Always worried about how things look." His previous American girlfriend was bulimic and only went to the beach to get a perfect tan. I listened carefully to his every word, determined to figure out what he wanted and to be that. Meanwhile, my arousal quotient spiked often and unpredictably, stimulated by fantasy where Carlos and I were heavy into each other; this inevitably led to a new and improved skill: masturbating when away from him, guilt-free. Weekends had evolved for more than studying.

My friend Leslie, when we were recovering from a run, shirts saturated with sweat, startled me by asking what Carlos and I have in common. A religious Catholic, she could be concerned that he's dating a Jewish girl, but she never said. I told her Carlos and I also love jogging, tennis, distance bicycling. She has seen us together on campus. Carlos told her he thinks I'm a super athlete! But privately, expressing concern with how much time I have been devoting to tennis, he warned me, "Stanford's hard; prepare, prepare, prepare." We did talk law some - he was obsessed with how blacks and Hispanics get screwed by the criminal justice system. "They get picked up and charged for no reason or for something no white guy would be. Then they can't make bail. Get a record so they can't get a job. Right out of apartheid!" I sympathized, but wondered how Carlos, who is determined to make it in criminal law - translation: mucho dinero - will help poor minorities who can't pay him to represent them? I didn't pursue the contradiction.

Watching Carlos in the courtroom acquainted me with a different aspect of this man. The reserved, at times withdrawn person I am getting to know did not exist there. In court the world sees a powerful force, articulate, confronting, precise. He's becoming the litigator he had dreamt he'd be, when as a youngster he watched his favorite old Hollywood trial movies with Gregory Peck and Spencer Tracy.

Outside the courtroom, Carlos was frantic with worry. He must pay his student loans, a car loan, his modest rent. He refused to let me buy dinner for us, accusing me of being the rich New Yorker who cannot understand how his parents and two sisters living in Cuernavaca, Mexico, have so little to show for their perpetual labors. He wanted to help them, anxious to fly home in December for his older sister's engagement party. My offer to help seemed to irritate him, so I shut up, hoping he'd invite me to join him. Carlos expressed no interest in my family. I bet he assumes I had had a perfect childhood. Yeah, right!

Early in the Fall semester, my mom called. We'd been in contact via emails and texts, with a few telephone calls where she seemed more together. Tonight was different.

"Human resources from your father's company telephoned. Did you know he took early retirement? He hasn't spoken to me in months. The money comes. I've been determined not to run after him. What does he say to you?"

My heart beating rapidly, I managed to admit not having heard from dad since early-May, four months. Mother was incredulous, sure I was lying to her. Then she started to cry. "Maybe he's sick, or even dead. Don't you care enough about him to wonder?" I felt terrible. What a rotten, self-absorbed daughter. Preoccupied.

Unconscious. She hurled adjectives at me faster than I could absorb them. I wanted to fight back, but deserved her scorn. How had it been possible to ignore his absence? A guilty thought: Both of you, leave me alone!

But my words hid that uncomfortable truth: "Mom, I'll look into it, I swear. I have some time before next semester begins. Did you call Dan Phelps?" Dad kept all their investments with Merrill Lynch, and had been close friends with his advisor for thirty years. So I thought Dan was likely to have dad's current address. Mom hadn't called Dan, and never opened statements because that was the way she typically dealt with money. So I urged her to fax me the last statement while we were talking. We were both startled by what it revealed. Dad had withdrawn exactly half of their assets, $1,134,840.

"Sally, I need you to come home. I can't handle this. Larry hates his father, so he refuses to talk to me when I mention his name. What am I going to do? Maybe we should hire a private investigator?"

"There is no way I can come home. You must manage. You're stronger than that. I will help, but from here. I promise. Don't ask me to give up law school. That's not fair. About an investigator, let's talk to Uncle Philip before doing anything."

She hung up.

Initially, Carlos was fascinated by my problem. Not so much supportive of me, but intrigued by the mystery of dad's disappearance. He offered suggestions after putting in some computer research on his own. I asked him for advice about hiring a private investigator. He thought that move was premature: "You know that'll cost a fortune - is your mom prepared for that? And your father may not want to be found."

One evening, observing me eyeballing a picture of his family taken before he headed to Stanford, Carlos practically accused me of being a racist. His dad and baby sister are darker-skinned, his mom and older sister appear to be white. His words shocked and infuriated me. I flung back a response: "How dare you accuse me of such a thing?" He shrugged on the way to the bathroom. We didn't revisit the issue.

Our relationship changed, though I wasn't conscious of just how much at the time. Maybe because I had become preoccupied. Or I needed him, asking for more of his time, more attention. He responded by being less available. How familiar is that?

In early December, Carlos travelled to Mexico for his older sister's engagement party. He hadn't given me a heads up beforehand. On his return, he acknowledged that he had never told his parents of my existence. I raged at him. He withdrew. I told him to go to hell, to drop dead, to fuck himself. He hung up on me. Though we got together twice more, neither of us was inclined to touch. We knew we were quits. It was such a painful time for me. I would have loved to believe it was equally painful for Carlos, but what I did believe: he experienced relief.

So the two important men in my life abandoned me. For days, I couldn't eat, went to class and studied alone, avoiding my group, slept, cried, raged in my room. I thought of sharing my grief with Elisa, with my aunt, with my new friend Leslie. But in a bizarre way I was proud to be suffering alone. I longed for the old Me, who never cared when relationships ended. How crazy is that? But it would have hurt less.

At my lowest point, I was shocked when at 1:10 am my doorbell rang incessantly. For a moment, I fantasized that Carlos had returned, desperately missing me. Boy, was I wrong.

Cousin Brett, whom I hadn't seen - or thought about - in over two years, arrived with his teenage girlfriend.

"What the fuck are you doing here - and at this ungodly hour?"

"Hey, cuz, you never used to talk like that. We need your help."

Ellen, a pale, too-thin 17 year-old who appeared much younger, immediately asked to use the bathroom. On her arm was a Walgreens' plastic bag filled with boxes of sanitary napkins.

"You'd better explain yourself!" Brett had a hangdog look as he responded: "Ellen's pregnant, hemorrhaging. Who needed this? I'm on probation, and she's a minor so I can't take her to Emergency."

"Nice. After years of no relationship with me, you thought I'd be delighted to rescue you. How the devil did you get my address?"

"My mom gave it to me. Of course I didn't tell her why I wanted it. She's so naive - she actually liked the idea that we'd finally reconnect."

"I don't blame Aunt Lily for who you are. And if I help you, it's because of loving her - I wouldn't do a thing for you. So get outta here, NOW!"

Before leaving, Brett said something to his girlfriend through the closed bathroom door. Then he thanked me. I ignored him.

So I ended up taking the kid to the closest Emergency, remaining in the waiting room studying while she was there for hours. Eventually, a nurse came out. The doctor wanted to see me. She referred to Ellen as "...your kid sister." I didn't contradict her. The doctor said her piece: "Your sister bled heavily after using a No. 10 knitting needle in an attempt to abort; the fetus is safe. Take her home, and fill the antibiotic prescription. Make sure she gets some rest. And she should see a shrink pronto, and an OB."

We called her parents at 6 am. I went to class. When I returned, Ellen was gone. She left me a note: "Thank you. I'll keep in touch." My thoughts went to: I hope not. And I never want to see Brett again.

If I hadn't been nuts before that damned visit, afterward I was even more off my game. But beginning a week later, my study mates pulled an intervention. They forgave my neglect, called me if I stood them up, dragged me to movies or dinners, all without asking questions I would not have welcomed. After all that drama, life reverted to bland. I did rejoin my regular tennis game and yoga, and eventually resumed running most mornings. Ironically, some pretty cool guys noticed me. I was not interested.

I had followed through on suggestions Carlos had made – that I call the King David Hotel in Jerusalem where dad stayed on those Israel trips, as well as contacting others who might know something. The hotel manager told me that dad had been there for one week, and had left on the date he had said would be his return to New York. El Al Airlines verified that dad had not canceled, but failed to use his return ticket.

Larry learned that our father had canceled purchase of the Escalade just days before leaving for Israel, and had never rented a condo in La Jolla, or purchased a new cabin cruiser. He must have known this at our last meeting; why lie to me? Even his brother Philip claimed ignorance. Can I believe my uncle?

Uncle Philip had been incarcerated for six months, so conversations were awkward. During Larry and mom's visit with him, they discussed whether to notify the NYPD or hire a private investigator. My uncle's position: "Sam could be into bad stuff. Wait to see what transpires. He may even contact one of us. But If you do decide to go ahead, be aware that international searches run $50-100,000. Alerting the NYC police could start trouble for Sam." We agreed to postpone either action.

So dad had lied to me during that Stanford visit. He planned to disappear but hadn't wanted us to know. Why? During my hour-long conversations with Larry and Uncle Philip, we went over the same territory before acknowledging that we couldn't come up with answers that made any sense to us. But what my uncle did accomplish was to arouse my anxiety to unmanageable, when he said, "I'm pretty sure my brilliant brother is up to no good." Naturally, Larry, always prepared to believe the worst about our father, expanded on this speculation. I was too distraught to mount an effective challenge.

Two friends noticed changes in me and volunteered their observations: Shannon asked, "What's going on? You've become a maniac on the tennis court, racing in front of me to grab my shots. I don't like it one bit!" Iris, with whom I am closer, expressed more of the same: "You are so obsessed with getting A's - showing off - you never shut up in class. People are talking. Give someone else a chance." Nice!

But my smartest friend, Leslie, was kinder: "I won't ask you anything - if you want to talk, I'm here for you. But you changed after your dad's visit, then more so after you broke up with Carlos. You need to talk to someone... " And, in her joking manner, "How much more weight can you afford to lose before you'll be mistaken for a scarecrow?" Ha!

Several friends tried to fix me up with a guy - but I had no interest. In fact, I told Leslie that I might enter a convent. For a few seconds, she took me seriously: "But aren't you Jewish?" Then we both laughed ourselves silly.

In spite of roiling depression and sleeping more than normal, I had managed to get good grades. In fact, since I had given up much social life, didn't watch films or read novels, I had more time to hit the books.

CHAPTER 4

The four year-old I had been, was often lonely, spending hours in front of my parents' bed talking to my dolls. Good at dialogue, I ended conversing when anyone was within earshot.

My imaginary friends, Jane and Mickey, were sick. That's why they never could get out of bed to play with me. Comforting them with pretend medicines, injections and juice, in return they loved me very much. I don't recall whether they contributed to the conversation.

Why had I been so lonely? My mother was nearby in the kitchen or laundry room, and Aunt Lily was in another apartment in my grandfather's fourplex. In a third apartment, there were two cousins, Edwin, two years older, and Naomi, a year younger, but we never played together. Mother felt my boy cousin was too wild, and his sister was severely retarded.

The house itself frightened me. For years after our family moved to our own Sea Cliff home, the house on Sparrow Lane fed my nightmares. I saw myself descending basement stairs facing a huge room painted Chinese red. Only visible from the bottom stair was a wide, tall cabinet in the same high gloss red. As I ventured into the room, its several doors leading to smaller off-limit rooms, the walls became alive with fire, threatening to engulf me. Screaming, I raced upstairs, only to awake in my own dark bedroom. Was anyone there to comfort me?

The small child I had been often watched my busy mother doing chores for the family. She cleaned and shopped, did loads of laundry, prepared feasts for her small brood and for the much larger family of which she was the matriarch. Everyone admired her. While I was at school, her friends came by for canasta or mah jongg. As I got older, I worried that she had too much work – but often I was upset with her because she didn't seem interested in making time to play with me.

There was a second mother on the scene, mom's much younger, prettier and livelier sister, Aunt Lily. She did everything for fun and best of all, loved to do it with me until I was four and she adopted a baby boy. Soon afterward, she moved away. I remember being so happy that her son became a very bad boy and a terrible student because I was a good girl and a great student. But Aunt Lily was certain that Brett would get better, and seemed less interested in how perfect I was. He never did get better, even got a lot worse. I eventually understood that his being a disappointment didn't make me any more important to her.

Remembering all this, I recalled that Aunt Lily and Uncle Bob had adopted another baby boy a year before Brett came; that baby died before he was six months old. Only three at that time, I thought they had given him away, but Aunt Lily told me years later that they had a funeral after he died of pneumonia. Ah, that may explain why I had play-acted caring for sick dolls.

I should have been happy to move away from that scary house, to have my own beautiful bedroom decorated in pink and white, plus a large, airy playroom with ping pong and loads of board games. But what I remember best about those days was having to say goodbye to my only real friend. Joy lived on Sparrow Lane. Because her mother never learned to drive, she couldn't bring her to our new house. Why didn't we talk by telephone? And why, since my mom had gotten her drivers' license before I was born, did she never take me to see my friend? Now I understand. Mom had been too scared that she might scratch daddy's car, so it never left the garage when he was on a business trip.

My dad traveled constantly once we went to war in Iraq. He was away so much that I mainly remember us dropping him off or picking him up at JFK. He returned with pretty ethnic dolls and what he called thinking games, like chess. When home, he played pinochle or poker with friends every Friday night. Mom worried that he might lose too much money, but he always came out even.

School was very easy for me. Making friends was much harder. It seemed that all the other children were bigger, and they knew things I hadn't learned, like what the penis was for besides peeing. One day, two girls teased me in the playground when I didn't know what 'intercourse' meant – this in third grade. I asked mom.

After that, I pretended to know everything so I didn't get teased again.

It's also possible the teasing stopped because I began buying candy to bring to school almost every day. Since my one dollar allowance wasn't enough, I took to stealing change from mom's wallet. She caught me and told me that her brother Jerry, who I hated, was a gambler and a thief. So I stopped stealing except for one last time, when I stole a Mickey Mantle baseball card from a friend on a playdate. Years later, when I learned it had become valuable, I searched, hoping to return it, without success.

My brother Larry is not often present in my memories of those childhood years. He's four years my senior, so was home until he left for Oberlin when I was thirteen. I have vague recollections of attending his recitals and of visiting him at camp and once at Oberlin.

Our dog Duchess was precious to my father from the moment he brought her home as an eight weeks' old puppy. We had dogs before her, like the cocker spaniel who followed me to school and got lost because I was afraid to bring him home and miss school. Duchess, with her fluffy white hair and big brown eyes, hated to be left alone even for a few hours. Of course, when our family took a long vacation to visit mom's parents in Florida, Duchess had to go into a kennel on Long Island. Once there, she stopped eating, forcing dad to fly home alone, then rent a car to drive our dog south. I was allergic to Duchess' shedding, leading my pediatrician to tell dad to get rid of her or I'd become asthmatic.

He fired the doctor; we kept the dog. Dad was right – I outgrew my allergies. My father and I walked Duchess together every evening whenever he was home. Those were precious bonding moments, as freed of the family drama, daddy was fun, with fascinating stories of far-off lands and amazing people.

Though only intermittently in New York, Sam Marcus had been and is still the dominant force in our small family, a reality accentuated with his whereabouts now unknown to us.

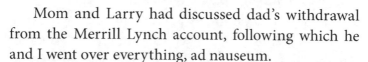

Mom and Larry had discussed dad's withdrawal from the Merrill Lynch account, following which he and I went over everything, ad nauseum.

"That bastard was planning to take off all along. We always knew he had affairs. Why, when he couldn't stand her, he stayed, is the real question. Mom's furious if I even allude to that. She pisses me off with her rewriting history. And she still is considering going to the police."

"Don't be so hard on her, Larry. She's humiliated and confused. I understand her better since Carlos dumped me. What does Elisa think?"

"She's shocked. She had begun to love dad. He flirted with her like he dealt with all women – and was so good at it. Imagine him disappearing so soon after we moved to New York. He pretended to be delighted to have a grandchild. Yeah, right. Full of shit, as usual. Elisa is hurt. She thought, what with her parents dead, Isabel would have loving grandparents if we moved here. And I joined her in that particular fantasy. Idiot me! So she's hurt, disappointed, miserable. And me, I'm disgusted at my own self-deception. *Stupidity!*"

"I'll grant you that daddy dealt with his leaving mom – and us – horribly. You were convinced that his divorcing mom was inevitable. They couldn't stand each other, like, forever. Yet mom sounds like she's lost the love of her life." After a joined silence, I spoke again:

"I don't get why he would have told me he'd be back for his birthday and that he ordered a new car and planned on buying a bigger yacht, on renting in La Jolla. Maybe he hadn't definitely planned on leaving. Maybe something bad has happened to him, forced his hand. Oh, my God, I don't know what to believe."

A sneering Larry responded: "How should we know what that self-indulgent creep was thinking? He may just have told you all that bullshit to throw us off." He lapsed into a brief silence. Then, "I should tell you that mom just gave us money for a downpayment on a two-bedroom co-op in Forest Hills. We're awaiting our interview with the Board. It's pretty nice, but needs work. You'll see it after the semester, even sooner, maybe."

I continued obsessing over possible reasons for dad's disappearance. Yes, he planned to leave; the money business made that obvious. When had he decided that and why? Might he have been blackmailed? That's nuts. He never seemed nervous when we were together last.

My thoughts went nowhere productive, only to more anxiety. Maybe I should see a therapist? Not yet. I have too much school work. Plus, is it so crazy to wonder why my father pulled this escape? Did he really elect to vanish - or was he kidnapped? Another crazy idea. Everything points to his executing a diabolical plan. He just could have divorced mom, split their money, and moved to Manhattan.

There's a lot we don't know. Do I want to know?

Ultimately, I decided that as long as my studies didn't suffer, I wouldn't go into therapy. All therapists do is drag you back to your childhood - when what I really need to do is to try to get some answers.

I bought a fancy, leather-bound notebook, planning to list what we know and what we need to know. It went into a bottom drawer in my dresser. And then I returned to my focus on class prep and volunteering at the local Legal Aid. My mantra: No Dating!

CHAPTER 5

A unt Lily picked me up at JFK after what had been a miserable flight, a barking dog and a couple of screaming kids constant irritants.

"Love you, baby," was her greeting, accompanied by a bear hug. Why did I begin crying?

"What's this all about, Sally?"

"Men disappearing, blaming us, so women who love them feel like shit."

Still hugging me, she acknowledged my pain, saying, "We women are stronger than these guys." Afterward, both silent, to my surprise she drove over the RFK bridge into Manhattan, exiting at 96th Street, where she parked in front of an Italian restaurant. The small, dark, artistically decorated near empty space was clearly a familiar haunt of hers. We studied our menus, sharing a carafe of sangria, postponing the conflict, which I anticipated.

"Sal, you know your mom's a mess. She should have divorced your dad years ago, but whatever either of us thinks, she never even entertained the possibility that he'd disappear."

"If I leave school at the end of this semester, I'll hate her! You have to keep out of this, Aunt Lily. Mom had no right to send you as her emissary to manipulate me into coming back here. And don't dare tell me she didn't."

"In fact, that's not why she asked me to pick you up. But how could you ever think I'd do such a thing? I'm hurt that you would believe it of me."

"I was afraid to make this trip. Three days with her is all I can stomach. She hates me. But why did you come? Elisa was supposed to."

"Isabel has a fever. Nothing serious, so don't worry. I wanted to see you alone anyway. About your mother. She's on the verge of doing something illegal, getting Ralph Klein to sign your father's name at a notary so she can sell the house. She bought a Manhattan condo – spending money like she's printing it. Sally, I think she's having a breakdown, but she refuses to see anyone who might help." If my aunt, mom's adored sister, can't influence mom, I certainly can't.

Before Aunt Lily dropped me off at the Sea Cliff house, she thanked me for helping Brett, then ignored my plea that she come in with me.

I was shocked by what confronted me. Both sides of the long entrance foyer were lined with professionally packed boxes. Gone were the sculptures and pictures. Post-its were on every item in the great room and den. Someone had written in black magic marker either FOR SALE and a price, or NFS, on everything. The elegant window treatments, mother's pride and joy, were gone, creating an exposed, eerie atmosphere. And where's Duchess? Margaret? Don't tell me she's gotten rid of them too.

She must have heard me come in, for suddenly there she is. I hadn't prepared myself sufficiently, even after the talk with Aunt Lily. Mom had lost the thirty pounds she had struggled with for years, yet she still was wearing her matronly grey a-line dress and was long overdue for a cut and color, her hair indifferently pulled back behind her ears.

"Mom, I didn't hear you." I kissed her, while she held me at arm's length. "What's going on here?"

"What does it look like? It's time. Your father's not coming back. What is an old woman living alone doing in a huge, isolated house? When Larry and Elisa moved, that's when I decided to sell this place."

"Don't you think you're making a rash decision? Or even if you eventually want to sell the house, is this the right time? And why are you thinking of yourself as old? You're what, 56?"

"What's your business, Sally? You don't want to be here either. You and Larry – you're both no help to me. Even worse, you're mean, hurtful."

"You wanted me to visit, didn't you? Please, mom, I can't leave school. And even if I could, these are decisions I don't know anything about. I respect that you're trying to figure things out without daddy. Maybe before you finalize this, you should consider seeing a therapist."

"That's your Aunt Lily's idea, isn't it? Listen, my asking you to come this weekend was so you can sort out your stuff, figure out what to keep, what to throw out or have me sell at next Sunday's tag sale. Then you can go back to where you belong."

My old bedroom had not been touched in years. It looked as it had since its redo while I was in high school. Strange that on rare weekends home from Barnard, I had never cared. Had I even noticed? Unable to sleep though near exhaustion, I tackled the task of going through stuff. Clothes not worn in years, pictures of movie or tennis stars (Serena, Rafey) - books I had admired as a teenager, all those I piled up outside the door. They would be sold or discarded. But then there were a few precious items: a gold and emerald ring given to me by my dad for my 16th birthday; a plaque after a significant Long Island tennis tournament, my first big victory; graduation pictures and yearbooks; and a diary, which at the time, I had hidden, fearful lest mom read it.

I sat on the carpeting – stained and a sickly pink – and read through that diary. My old worry about it had me giggling. Nothing shocking there. Just normal kid fantasies about love and sex, along with a few hostile cracks about my mother. Why hadn't I put in anything about Uncle Bob? Wondering this, I checked the last date. It was on the winter I turned fourteen, just months before that summer.

The weekend visit with mom didn't get any better. She never came out of her room for breakfast, never suggested we dine out together. I overheard her talking to her mother, who had recently moved into assisted living in Boca Raton; when I asked to speak to grandma, my mother ignored me. She couldn't wait to get rid of me on Sunday.

Before leaving New York, I did get to visit with Elisa and Isabel. Larry was off on a weekend's gig. Isabel was out of sorts with a head cold and ear infection. Elisa, three months pregnant, excited to see me when I had called from California, was wrung out after having been awake at night with her daughter. So she was not up for our usual intimate visit.

Duchess had been living here, showing her age (12) but she perked up at my visit. We cried together at our reunion.

From Elisa, "I can't get too involved just now. Your brother is still not back to normal, and is away with his band most weekends. He hates teaching, and at times I think he hates me too for agreeing to move here. He's only his old self with Isabel."

"I'm so sorry, Elisa. You don't deserve my crazy family."

At Terminal 5 JFK far earlier than necessary and in a near dream-like state, a troubling Sally/Mom memory forced itself into my thoughts.

Believing myself beautiful on that sparkling May evening, all done up for my high school prom date with Jimmy, I strolled down our staircase to await my father's picture-taking. Friend Natalie had helped me pick out a stunning fitted, shimmering, orchid gown, and had come over to do my make-up and at least attempt to style my curly bob. She accompanied me downstairs. My parents were waiting, looking up at us, with dad smiling his approval. Then mom spoke her viciousness:

"You look like a whore in that dress. Take your boobs out all together, why don't you?" She left us.

I didn't feel sad or hurt, but despised her, and said as much to Natalie, who hugged me before leaving, no doubt shocked. When my date arrived, corsage in hand, dad accompanied us to the limo with my overnight bag; he whispered, "Your mom didn't mean it - she can be crazy at times." My furious, whispered response: "Do Not Defend Her!"

For two weeks afterward, I left any room she entered. She followed me, tried to apologize; I could not forgive her. Can I ever?

CHAPTER 6

Back at Stanford, and in spite of my need to prep for finals, I set up a midday meeting with one of the partners at the law firm where I had interned last summer. She was gracious, while I, struggling to present a professional self, must have seemed frantic. Over coffee – she had lunch at her desk – I reviewed what little I had learned and asked for her advice. She initially thought the family might benefit from hiring a private detective if the family could afford the expense, but changed her mind when I indicated that dad was likely in Israel or another country - definitely not anywhere in the U.S.

That meeting led to my contacting an executive at dad's former employer, J.J. Richfield & Co. Dad had worked there my whole life, VP in charge of domestic sales for this machine tool manufacturing company. The man heading the marketing department verified that dad had taken early retirement, much to the company's surprise and distress.

"Sam was very valuable to us. We never expected him to leave so soon. Because management had an idea that he had been offered more money elsewhere, we upped his commission. But he was adamant, hell-bent on retiring. He assured us that he would not work for a competitor, though we did not have a non-compete agreement at that time. He also denied being ill. We asked him to stay long enough to break in his replacement."

"Did he?"

"To some degree. He made a last swing around the country with his runner-up, introducing him to our customers. And he attended his retirement luncheon. Did he show you his Tag Heuer? He was pretty happy with it, and with his bonus, almost a half-million dollars."

The executive's comments reflected his surprise at how little he had known dad after working with him for over twenty years. This followed my filling him in on recent developments, certain he'd tell others at the firm who might know something helpful.

Naturally, law students get to be pretty good at doing research, and I was no exception. Since that disturbing visit with mom, I had been calling hospitals and police departments in various locations that dad frequented, as well as his New York physician and banker/friend at Chase. I learned that dad had been in excellent health, though somewhat overweight – that I knew – and that neither man had any advance warning of dad's plan to leave. Both were reluctant to share more – assuming they knew anything else – citing confidentiality.

Two other calls were a little more productive. The one to Uncle Philip, mystified and disturbed me.

"Sally, my girl, great hearing from you. Look, I have only a few minutes to talk. Have a date I'd rather not have to keep. But it's a helluva lot better than prison. Your uncle is on probation for a year."

"Sorry about your trouble, Uncle Philip. You know I'm calling about dad again. Larry and I believe, if anyone knows anything, it would be you."

"Your father was one mysterious dude. Of course I always knew about the women. Since I'm far from an angel myself, I never judged him. That is, not until your cousin Gerald told me about Sam's visit to Toronto. That would be two years ago, months before he left." Uncle Philip lapsed into a rare silence before volunteering, "My brilliant brother, why the devil did he bring a lady friend to the Israel Independence Day celebration? They bumped into Gerald and his family at the parade, ended up having dinner together. To quote Gerald: 'She's a nice person, friendly, smart too. Not a looker. She invited us to visit anytime.'"

"I can't believe dad was so stupid! And Gerald, what did he have in mind?" Angry tears streamed down my cheeks. Then it was my turn to be silent, until I got an idea: "I want that woman's address and telephone number. I'm calling Gerald."

"There's another story you might want to know about. Over drinks at my club, shortly after your parents returned from their trip to Spain three years ago, your mother complained about Sam's behavior on the trip. They had travelled there with the Levines, and were having a great time until they got to the Costa del Sol. Sam wanted Rhoda to stay at the hotel with their friends while he hydro-foiled to Morocco. He was insistent. So was she. Sam couldn't stop Rhoda from going, but ignored her on the boat trip there. Then, during their stroll around the market, without a word your father took off. Naturally Rhoda was very nervous in that frenetic place alone, so she stayed put, sitting on a stool one of the vendors provided. Sam returned in twenty minutes, all smiles. He made up some cock and bull story about having a long chat with a man who sold electronics. He claimed to be sorry that he hadn't warned your mom. As usual, he refused to answer any of her questions, then dragged her off to an Oriental rug gallery to distract her."

"When did she tell you that story? I remember their trip, but not a word about that Morocco caper."

"It was before I was indicted. My brother was late in meeting us. While waiting for Sam, Rhoda told me about Sam's passport. She had seen it just before their trip. It had dozens of stamps from travel to countries he never had told her he visited. When Sam discovered her with his passport, he was furious, acted like she did something wrong. Eventually, he told her that he'd been working on secret projects for the firm, and could only share on a 'need to know' basis. She didn't believe him. She was convinced he had a girlfriend somewhere in the Middle East. That was a crock – but I had no other explanation so didn't bother contradicting her." Uncle Philip offered one final observation: "My brother sucks as a liar. No one with a brain would believe his crazy stories. And you should know that when I asked Sam what the hell was going on, he told me to mind my own business. He was up to something illegal. That's why I told you all not to bring on the cops or a detective."

Naturally, after this new information, I had to call dad's former colleague again, apologizing for bothering him. He was gracious, saying he owed it to my father's family to do whatever he could to be of help.

"What Middle East countries did my father cover for the company?"

"None, specifically. We have a foreign division. And you probably know that our government strictly regulates what we can and can't sell to foreign governments. We provide our military with state of the art electronics. We can sell, with restrictions, to Israel, Egypt, Saudi Arabia, Jordan and to our NATO allies. Do you remember reading about BAE Corp selling products to the Saudis after the U.S. Congress prohibited the sale? I can't be sure, but will look into whether your dad was ever asked to take on projects in those countries. Can you hold?"

Mr. Jenson verified that dad had on several occasions conducted business in Israel during the four years prior to his retirement, his fluency in Hebrew and Israel contacts considered assets. Though never asked to personally handle projects in Egypt or Jordan, he had joined a team from the firm to travel to these countries at least once, and had been sent to Bahrain with his boss to consult on repairs of previously purchased items.

With dad's travel expense reports in front of him, Mr. Jenson was able to give me the dates of his various Middle Eastern trips.

Following our conversation, I called Larry, who had obtained dad's canceled passport from his locked office desk. I was impressed that my brother had smashed the lock, this with mom's permission. Afterward, Larry and I compared notes from our differing vivid memories, which at times were stimulated by passport stamps.

As Larry is four years older than me, he was able to recall more of dad's earlier comings and goings, his presents on returning, even our mother's suspicious rants. But those trips were "normal" - authorized by his company, or vacations with family.

More recent passport entries listed trips which had been authorized by J.J. Richfield & Co. But that canceled passport had been replaced - and the new one is undoubtedly in dad's possession. Larry insisted we must share what we learned with our mother. "She's entitled. And maybe it'll help her to emotionally divorce him."

CHAPTER 7

I n the midst of all this stress, after finals my friend Amy asked me to join her on a ski trip to Vail over the Christmas holiday. She had her own skis and boots, and tried her hardest to manipulate me into buying. I resisted, will rent. She gave in, happy I agreed to join her, then booked us at an upscale, in-town Vail resort, fireplace and soaking tub in rooms. That won me over. If I am rotten at skiing, I'll hang out in the spa. She smirked, rolled her eyes, stuck out her tongue. "Coward!"

So here we are, after flying into Denver during a light snowfall, overnighting, the following day travelling by minivan in heavier snow during the two hours to our hotel. Nothing scares Amy. I was shaky.

Vail Mountain Lodge has the expected holiday decorations, their guests milling around dressed in stunning one-piece ski suits and fur boots, speaking German, French and Italian, along with English. Most include families with young kids and teens wearing their own snazzy ski outfits. Amy fit right in. Me, I was wearing a black down parka and old ski pants. Maybe my friend was right, when she ordered, "Shop!"

We're here for a week, having signed up for multi-hours' daily group ski lessons in one of three small, skill-appropriate groups. I'm a novice, while Amy insists she's an expert. She and I are so different; I wanted to register as a beginner, though I've skied occasionally for years. She filled out her form, emphasizing her expertise and style. I couldn't resist kidding her: "Try out for our Olympic team, why don't ya?" After signing our rights away, we were set for different groups.

Dinner is amazing, less for the food, than for the ambience. We're seated at a window overlooking Town Center, next to a large round table occupied by foreign tourists. We eavesdrop without shame, but soon are invited into their conversation. I expressed surprise that so many Europeans, surrounded by the Alps in their various home countries travel to Colorado for ski vacations. And I'm in awe that the ten year-old girl nearest me addresses her parents in German, speaks French to her younger sibling, and English to me. Her parents, in great shape and acknowledged expert skiers, tell me that ski conditions here are superior to their local slopes, and fees, meals, etc., even in our upscale lodge are more affordable than in their countries.

The German couple invited me to check out the nearest low intermediate slope, which they are convinced will be the one my class begins on tomorrow. Tall, husky Eric pointed up at the slope: "Look, it's gorgeous, aren't you excited?" I admitted to being more nervous than excited, after which his wife, Jena, told me, "Your instructor will be fabulous! You'll be skiing like a pro before the week's out." Before we went our separate ways, Eric asked me about President Trump. "We Germans have always admired the U.S., now we don't know." Well, neither do we. I love Angela Merkel, sad she's soon to leave politics.

I overslept this morning after a restless night. Amy was not happy. So I hurried to get ready, arriving at a late breakfast. We seated ourselves at an empty large round table, carrying pancakes, sausages, juice and coffee from the buffet. Then I see him, heading our way.

He would normally not be all that noticeable, as he is of medium height and build, but his expressive, dark eyes, shining behind steel-rimmed glasses, focused on me. He smiled, sitting far across from us. Conversation was near impossible as many guests mill around, picking up gear before heading out for the slopes. I imagined that the man, Jonah, was expecting his wife or girlfriend. But no, he ate quickly, offering, "Have a nice day," before leaving.

At five, Jonah joined me in our lobby where wine was being served. The crowded sofas all faced an enormous stone fireplace.

"You seem so animated, Sally." Admittedly I was pumped. Running from troubles works.

"Oh, I'm relieved – and happy to see you again. My group has a wonderful instructor, a tiny thing, years ago on the French Olympic ski team. Imagine my luck having her. We have some good skiers in our group, mainly teenagers. I didn't do as poorly as I had anticipated." What I did not volunteer was my relief at not hitting the wall – altitude sickness – which felled at least one of the teens in my group.

We spoke for a few minutes before Amy joined us.

Conversation seemed to focus on how the Europeans manage to consume so much wine and still ski like pros. Amy left us – perhaps sensing Jon and I might like some alone time – or maybe she spied some attractive guy.

This became an amazing vacation. Great weather, fun skiing with my fellow downhillers (who treat me as their big sister), and off-slope time with Jon. Though Amy, Jon and I have meals together, afterward he and I go off on our own. On our fifth day, he spied me as I hung up my skis, insisting that we go into the communal outdoor hot tub. "Sally, you can do it! Everyone has to. It's a rite of passage for skiers." I had fought him on previous days, but afterward had to admit it was terrific. Though others were around, he found a private spot, and kissed me, not for the first time. Holding me against him, moving away, he joked, "This is not exactly the right place to get aroused!" I couldn't help giggling. Without another word between us, we left.

Jon had his own room. Heading there, I joked, "You must be rich not to have a roommate – either that or you planned on an assignation." He ignored my crack, while taking off my sweater and pulling my bathing suit top down to my waist. We kissed, touching in private places. Then, to my surprise and disappointment, he pulled back. I wanted to ask if he was going for a condom, but – no – he just released me. Maybe he doesn't like my body or find me exciting enough. Maybe he's engaged or even married back in Chicago. My distrust quotient rising, I decided to return to my room to grab a quick nap, ending Jon's comment in mid-sentence.

The next evening we were with a lively crowd, dancing on the multi-colored lighted square to a terrific rock band, many doing some serious drinking, others smoking weed, legal here. We were also somewhat intoxicated via the free-flowing wine, but were not interested in smoking. Jon drew me to a quieter place, only to startle me with the suggestion that I come home with him for the long New Year's weekend. When I reminded him that I am to join my friend Amy at her parents' in Sarasota, he grimaced: "You can go a couple of days later. I'm booking you on my flight to Chicago." I didn't say no. So he did.

Amy was troubled, lecturing me: "I'm worried about you, Sal. Do you know what you're doing? Everyone hooks up here, drinks a lot, dances, gets laid, then they go home to the real people in their lives. You don't have a clue who he is!" She could be right. And she thinks I haven't gotten over Carlos. I like Amy, but she's one bossy broad.

During the Chicago flight, I privately revisited the question of why Jon had interrupted our lovemaking. And I asked myself whether I am all that attracted to him, or more attracted to his interest in me.

Once in his small Lake Shore Drive condo, he initiated an explanation.

"I've only been single for two years. My wife died of liver cancer. My best buddy thinks it's about time I deal with how lonely I am – he pushed me to this trip. I wasn't sure I was ready, but didn't want to be alone for the holidays. And then we met."

I noticed his late wife's pictures, one with Jonah and their dog, hanging on the wall over the hall table. She was a striking brunette, with long, straight hair and prominent cheekbones. There was an unquestionable facial resemblance to me, and, she appeared to be about my height and build. Jon noticed where my attention had strayed.

"What's on your mind, Sally?"

"Were you struck with my resemblance to your wife when we first met? There's no way you can miss it."

"Is my being attracted to petite, gregarious, smart women a deficit? You sound suspicious, as if you think I see you as a potential replacement."

"Look, I appreciate that you are still mourning your wife. That you are working on re-entering the social scene. I just don't want to be a transitional vehicle for anyone's recovery. I had a bad break-up myself. So I am suspicious." After a pause, I added, "And you should be too."

We walked into his living room, seating ourselves on the sectional couch at some distance from each other. A neighbor chose that moment to come by with Jonah's tiny white poodle. The woman, Moira, had taken care of the dog while Jon was away. So there were introductions and chatting, while Jon and I were likely both distracted by our concerns, and by the dog jumping all over him. When Moira left, we resumed our conversation. Because he didn't want to leave Angel so soon after their reunion, Jon ordered in. We then ran her outside. On our return to the apartment, he spoke:

"Look, I know we're geographically incompatible right now, but I hope we find a way to get to know each other better, and if we do get close, you would consider taking the Illinois bar and relocating here." He was way, way ahead of me. Why was he in such a hurry? And my always-present internal question, Why would this guy (any guy?) be so attracted to me?

Jon didn't seem fazed by my shrugging response. Instead, he kissed me, taking his time to undress me while we were still standing at the entrance to his bedroom, his back against the doorframe. I felt him hard against me, and was aware of my own wetness. I fully cooperated, pulling his tight jeans over his unyielding penis. He helped, throwing his jeans, shoes and underwear toward the bed, saying, "You're beautiful. I love your dark, curly hair, on your head and down below." He laughed as some strands got into his mouth. Just before he entered me, I told him that I'm not on the pill. Does he have a condom? I got that he's pleased that I'm not promiscuous. He brought me to a climax orally, which delighted him. He allowed me to do the same for him. Then moving away for a moment, accessing his dresser, he returned with a condom. We kissed, eyes open, me wanting to reach behind his gaze. Aroused again, he put on the condom and entered me.

The next day, in between lovemaking, we ate and we slept. We never discussed any future plans, which was a relief to me and perhaps to him. He knew that I had to fly to Sarasota the following morning, and didn't challenge me though he had two more vacation days.

At the airport, he acknowledged that he was nervous too. "It's because we've gotten so close so fast."

I asked him about his religion. He laughed. "Jonah Segal? What else could I be but Jewish? My parents are sabras. I grew up in Israel." He asked me about my own religious background: definitely Reform. I sensed, but did not follow up on, his open disappointment that I didn't automatically join him in taking Israel's side about their expanding settlements, and the moving of our Embassy to Jerusalem. Jon is diplomatic: "Let's agree to disagree. You haven't lived in Israel, so how can you know what it's like to negotiate with the hardline religious right." It's difficult for me to be silent: "Netanyahu's a criminal, and his being Trump's pal does nothing to warm me to him."

Coward that I am, I had promised to spend several days with Amy's family in Sarasota, Florida. She picked me up at the airport. Surprising, given her personality, Amy asked me no questions about my Chicago adventure. She seemed a bit cool, leaving me wondering whether she would have preferred my canceling.

But her family was welcoming. At meals, everyone focused on her brother's twin boys and the plentiful, if uninspiring food. The warm weather allowed us to spend hours at the community's pool, and to power-walk and ride bikes. What a treat, particularly so after Colorado and Chicago weather. Never having been to Sarasota, I was impressed by my reading of the town's cultural offerings in their local newspaper, then amused when Amy volunteered that her parents weren't "...too interested in concerts or ballet. They love bridge, golf and eating out."

In this family there was no adult conversation. I apparently erred by asking questions about Florida's politics. Her dad's response: "We don't discuss serious issues here!" For Amy, that's normal. She jumps right in, volunteering about recent films, restaurants, discount malls. Is it possible that I might prefer my intense, argumentative brethren?

Jonah had called to check on my safe arrival, and to wish me a happy new year. Having planned to stay home until his friends insisted on his joining them at a small party, Jonah admitted that joining in local celebrations was still difficult. But he's pushing himself to do just that.

CHAPTER 8

Back on campus before classes resume, I found the courage to call Betty Rand. She answered on the first ring, responding to my announcement, "I'm Sam Marcus' daughter, Sally," with equanimity.

"Hello. I've heard so much about you, but never expected to hear from you. What can I do for you?"

"You can tell me where my father is. Does he live with you?"

"I haven't heard a word from Sam in two years. We were, ah, good friends, for almost ten years, so I was troubled when he stopped keeping in touch. Without any notice, either. But then, well, I got to thinking he decided against leaving his wife, your mother."

"Did he tell you he was planning to leave her? That he'd be with you?"

"Yes to the first, no to the second. Sam spoke about his unhappy marriage and for years told me he'd leave after your high school graduation. Then he didn't, did he? For sure, he never promised to marry me, or even to live with me. What he did say was after his divorce, he'd retire and we'd travel together. That happened once, to Canada, as you must know."

"I'd like to meet you. I have a friend in Chicago. You live about two and a half hours' train ride. Can we agree on a visit?"

"Sally, I owe you that. While I never felt all that guilty about your mother, because Sam was so unhappy, I did think about you – about the effect of his eventually leaving the family on such a young girl. Please come. I'll email you directions, and you let me know when you can make the trip. I teach at UI, Urbana-Champaign, but I never teach on Fridays, and am typically home by 4 pm on other weekdays.

I had booked the train from Chicago's airport on this dreary, cold, snowy mid-January Friday. The tightness in my chest that had persisted during the flight from San Francisco to Chicago had dissipated. What was left was a kind of numbness. Why go? The train ride offered a welcome dullness, which was temporarily interrupted by two young Argentinian girls anxious for information; they spoke little English. I used my marginal high school Spanish to some effect, then promised myself to upgrade both Spanish and French – someday.

Betty is older, around 50, and plump, simply dressed, with little makeup, nowhere the glamour girl I had imagined. She exuded warmth in greeting me at the entrance to her modest, charming cape. I liked her – against my will, conscious of feeling a traitor to my mother.

"Welcome! I've seen pictures of you when you were a teeenager. Your father was so proud of your accomplishments in school and with tennis." She added that dad had told her that he had more trouble with his son, and had used her "… as a sounding board, not very successfully."

Following Betty into her modest all white kitchen with its sliding glass door leading out to the snow-covered brick patio, I marveled that my materialistic dad would be attracted to such simplicity. Betty insisted on serving her meat loaf specialty with fried sweet potatoes – a delicious meal she had prepared for me, one she called "…your dad's favorite."

As we ate, Betty shared something of her history with my father. "Sam told me when we first met that he was national sales manager for an electronics firm based in Chicago, that he traveled a lot. He was open about being married. From the first, I learned not to ask questions. We had met at a Chicago hotel bar the night my divorce was finalized, so I was feeling a mixture of relief and anxiety. That's probably why I, like Sam, was quite content with his periodic visits. He'd call – announcing he'd be in town the next day – always assuming I'd be free. I made myself free for him. Otherwise, he did keep in touch by phone or with cards from exotic places. I kept those – would you like to see them?"

I nodded before she continued. "For reasons I don't fully understand, in the year leading up to his disappearance, I found myself missing him, in love with him. I wanted more. But never said anything. Once he was gone, I assumed he was running from me."

So dad had also been dishonest with this kind

woman. I felt compelled to reassure her: "Betty, if it makes you feel any better, my father wasn't lying about his marriage. Mother is a wonderful homemaker – intelligent, responsible, but not much fun. Angry a lot. Whether she was so angry before she found out that dad cheated on her, who knows? Maybe dad did love you. He's up to something you had nothing to do with. We don't have a clue yet. But we're working on it."

"Since you've been so generous with me, Sally, I must return the favor. Your father never wanted to go to Toronto with me. I had been planning to visit my sister in Hamilton – a short distance from Toronto, and pleaded with him to join me. He was reluctant. Once we were there, he decided to attend the Israel Independence Day celebration in town. He imagined there would be thousands to protect us from bumping into family. Well – a shock – we met his nephew almost immediately. That nice young man implored us to join them for dinner. All in all, it was a fine evening, except that your aunt was unfriendly. She ignored both of us. Before we left the restaurant, Gerald asked me for my address as he was to attend a conference in Chicago the following month. I gave it to him. He never called. Sam was uptight that whole evening. He worried that his sister would tell your mother."

"Someone did tell mom." Always on the prowl, that could have been true, or she may have checked his phone bill. Mom once admitted to me that she on one occasion had dad followed; that's how she originally learned about the other 'courvas,' which is what she called his women. That means tramp in Yiddish. Betty is no courva!

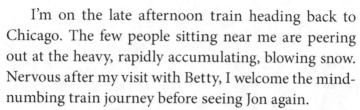

I'm on the late afternoon train heading back to Chicago. The few people sitting near me are peering out at the heavy, rapidly accumulating, blowing snow. Nervous after my visit with Betty, I welcome the mind-numbing train journey before seeing Jon again.

I can't help but notice an elderly gentleman accompanied by who appears to be his attentive, adult daughter, sitting diagonally across from me in this shabby train car. Two thirty-something men with expensive briefcases, staring at their iPhones, chat briefly in between calls. But it's a mother with two young daughters who hold my attention. I strain to hear what the older of the two, 8 or 9 years-old at most, is saying. The impatient child raises her voice: "How long is this boring trip anyway? How come we couldn't fly? Why didn't daddy come with us?"

Shifting my gaze from out the fogged window, I experienced a physiological change affecting my arms, my chest, and legs. I'm frozen in this stifling train, shivering in spite of my down jacket, mittens and woolen hat. And I am exhausted.

I somehow become that eight year-old with my mother on that original train trip. She's whispering, though no one sits near us. She tells me we are going to Boston. Daddy had driven us there the previous summer on that trip to Martha's Vineyard. This is different. It's winter. And I don't want to hear what mom's saying, but she repeats her words: "She can't do this to me, to us!" She is angry and tells me that we're going to see a bad woman who wants to take daddy away from us. I asked her if the woman will be mean, but she ignores me. She keeps talking, now in a loud whisper so I don't have to strain to hear her. She says daddy did a very bad thing. "I won't take it from him anymore. If he doesn't get his act together, he'll never see you again."

Now I'm crying and mommy apologizes. "I shouldn't have said that; it's just that I'm so upset, I don't know what I'm saying." I ask her, "Was I bad, mommy? Is that why he won't see me? Won't he come home after his business trip?"

Mommy says she doesn't know if he's coming home. How can that be? He always comes and brings stuff, presents for me, the last time a shawl for grandma, a new leather wallet for Larry. Once he brought mommy a mink scarf that she wears to go out when it's special. So daddy will come home, won't he?

Now she's quiet and says we're to read our books. She bought me a Judy Blume novel. Then we're off the train. At the station we eat hot dogs with mustard and sauerkraut. Mommy drinks coffee and buys me orange juice. Afterward we go out where it's even colder than New York. There's snow on the ground. We get a cab right away. Mommy tells me to be quiet because I keep asking her where we're going. She says, "To meet daddy's girlfriend." She says her name: Vicki. Mommy looks so mad, I'm scared of her. Soon the cab stops in front of a brownstone on Commonwealth Avenue, and we get out, with mommy telling the driver to wait with the meter running. We'll be back soon.

An old lady lets us in without our ringing the doorbell. It's Saturday, so mommy is sure Vicki will be home. A pretty, tall lady wearing a BU sweatshirt and jeans answers her door. At first she seems nice, but when mommy pushes her way into the apartment and says her name, Vicki tells us to leave: "Get out or I'll call the police! You have some nerve coming here and threatening me. What do you want?"

Mommy is shouting now: "I want you to leave my husband alone! This is my little girl. She's only eight and needs her father." Now she's crying and screaming at the same time. Vicki gets right up close to mommy's face and screams back: "Get out of here NOW!" She tries pushing mommy out the door.

I beg mommy: "Can I go to the bathroom. I gotta go, mommy, please." Ignored, I wet my pants. The pee goes on the lady's wood floor and on the corner of her pretty rug. No one pays attention to me, so It all comes out and I'm soaking wet. Crying, "Let's go, mommy, please!"

We get into the waiting taxi. I'm scared to wet the man's seat, whisper that to mommy. At first she doesn't seem to hear me. Finally, she says, "We'll buy you new pants before the train."

I'm not thinking anymore about mommy and that lady, just about my wet tights and pants and what if the cab driver notices that I smell bad. Mommy says we are to never talk about today, ever. It's our secret.

We do go to Filene's, where I get an entire new snowsuit and underwear; then, surprising me, we enter the toy department, where mommy buys me a baby doll and a large bear. Near the cashier, she spies playing cards, which she also buys. "We'll play rummy on the train." That didn't happen. But we did go to the store's restaurant, where mommy let me order whatever I wanted once the waitress noticed us. She never said a word to me during that meal, so I talked to my new doll. I told her that she was going on a long train trip and we'd soon be home.

Returning to the present with difficulty, I managed to rise, pressured by actually having to pee, then stumbled clumsily past the few seated, preoccupied passengers, to enter what is a smelly Amtrak bathroom at the far end of the train car. Tears, up until then contained, travelled down my cheeks. I remained in the bathroom until multiple knocks forced my exit.

Thinking back to my recent perusal of my diary, I wonder why I never spoke of the traumatic meeting with daddy's then girlfriend, or even wrote about it in my diary. But I knew the answer: I kept my mother's terrible secret, even from myself, no matter the ultimate damage to me. The eight year old child hadn't consciously decided to protect her, but she may have understood that her mother was ashamed, which was why she had asked her daughter to keep the trip secret.

How weird that I think of the child I was as 'she'.

It's as if there was a split in me between the before and after that trip.

How to get past the insidious distrust I have for my mother - for my father - and for anyone else who tries to get close to me? That frightening thought invaded my being, not for the first time, during the taxi ride to Jonah's.

CHAPTER 9

J onah's tiny Maltepoo greeted me enthusiastically on my arrival at his immaculate, stark white condo. Angel jumped on me repeatedly, hoping for a walk, but I was in no condition to fight the storm.

I must speak to my mother before Jon returns from work. Keeping my down jacket on until the apartment's warmth took over, I opened a bottle of cabernet and downed a full glass before placing that call.

Mom initially sounded so happy to hear from me.

"This is no casual call, mom. I must see you in person, and soon, but I've had a difficult time of it today and must talk now."

"I'm listening, dear. What's the matter? I'm so sorry about how I was when you came home. Lily was right. I had a meltdown. So I did get antidepressants from my internist and feel much better. Of course I plan to come for graduation. We all are."

"We'll talk about that another time. I need you to come immediately! There's no waiting for months. Don't let me down. I'm glad you're feeling better. Well, I'm not. I spent the afternoon with a woman who was daddy's girlfriend for ten years."

"What? How can that be? Is he with her now? Does she know where he is? Oh, my God."

"No, on either count. He did a disappearing act

on her too. She's a very decent woman. I know you'd prefer my telling you she's a bitch, a tramp, anything but what she really is. She's divorced for many years, teaches sociology at a university near Chicago. She loved daddy."

"Do you think I want to hear this? I knew for years that your father was unfaithful, but I never imagined that he had an ongoing relationship with another woman. I thought he just moved from tramp to tramp."

"No, you didn't mom. Remember our little trip to Boston to confront that young woman. I was eight years-old, right? It all came back to me today. Why, why would you have ever taken a young child on such a trip? What kind of a mother were you, anyway?"

"I've always felt so guilty about that trip, Sally. It was horrible to do that to you. And maybe worse, to never, ever speak to you about it. I hoped you'd forget it, like children do, and, selfishly, I was relieved that you never mentioned it. That is, until your Aunt Lily told me that I committed a crime against a child. How's that for directness?"

"She was right. We have a lot more to talk about, things I never shared with you. And things you might have guessed, but never acted as if you knew. I'm leaving Chicago, returning to Stanford on Sunday evening. I expect you to come out west next Friday. We'll stay in a hotel near campus."

"I could come before that if you like."

"No, I have a paper for Law Review due, and am

involved with a complicated case at the Legal Aid office. I hope I can handle everything."

After hanging up, I found myself perspiring heavily, seeking the sanctuary of the guest shower. When Angel cried to join me in the bathroom, I'm ashamed to admit that I screamed at her: "Get lost!"

Afterward, I crawled under the covers in Jon's bed. Angel jumped up, assuming her normal spot. She found the farthest corner, repelling my effort to push her off the bed.

Jon arrived home two hours later, anticipating a romantic reunion. Instead, he found me prone, asleep in his bed. I awakened with his kissing my forehead. His first words: "You seem to have a fever." Dr. Jon took wonderful care of me, until, celibate throughout the weekend, we separated at O'Hare on Sunday evening.

CHAPTER 10

The troubling strong odor of nearby forest fires accompanied us as we registered at a modest bed and breakfast near campus. Seated, shivering, drinking coffee outside a Starbucks, mom looks tired, also nervous. She had spoken nonstop since arriving, whether about the treacherous California fires or of her fellow passengers on the long flight from New York, I'm sure anxious of what was in store for her. Coffees and cranberry muffins allowed us to briefly retreat into trivia. Where to begin?

I feel sorry for her but more so for me. She has no clue what I'm about to tell her, and I have only a vague idea why I need to share this now after so many years of silence. Maybe I'm sick of family secrets. And I fear for precious Isabel. That alone justifies the telling.

"Mom, I'm glad you made it. I know you've been through so much, what with dad leaving, selling the house, our estrangement. But unless we do this, it's not clear what kind of relationship we'll have going forward." Taking a deep breath, watching my mother's face for clues, I await her response. We're both shivering – but neither of us suggests we enter the restaurant.

"Sally, I know we've been out of sorts with one another on and off since your teens. You never would talk to me. You seemed to prefer anyone else. Aunt Lily;

your friend Catherine's mother. I thought it was your age. That it would pass. Maybe now I'll finally learn the whys from you."

"If you had ever asked, I might have told you. Where shall I start? Should it be when I knew you were using me to hold onto daddy? That I became a flirt, hanging around him in a revealing bikini, hugging him so inappropriately that he put a stop to it? Or perhaps when I decided that you hated me. I was about twelve then. You say I stopped talking to you. I remember it the other way around. You were always criticizing, correcting what I said, how I said it, what I wore, how my hair looked. Some of my friends thought you were jealous of me. I had read a Judy Blume novel where the mother acts like you did, and that's how it came out in the story – the mother's jealousy because the father loved his daughter and not her. After reading that book, I felt better. I thought you're the crazy one; there's nothing wrong with me."

When my frozen mother offered to get us more coffee – indoors - I agreed. We needed the break. As we entered, a young couple, who had noticed us sitting outdoors, eyeballed us as they passed on their way out, I'm sure thinking we're two crazies.

Mom, on returning with fresh coffee, started to say something, then thought the better of it. I know if she had been defensive, it would have fueled my old anger. So she's smarter than I've often given her credit for, in choosing silence.

"Were you really ignorant of Uncle Bob's trying to rape me?"

"What? Don't tell me you think I knew anything that awful and didn't do something. What happened? When? Why didn't you ever tell me?"

Mom's color changed, her pale face blotchy, her hand holding coffee shaking.

"The first time I can remember was when I was eleven. I had just gotten my period and started wearing a training bra. He grabbed me in our hall while everyone was still at dinner, smelling from booze. He touched my breast, rubbed his penis on my leg. It was disgusting. I pushed him, and when he let go of me, I ran into my room. After that night, I kept away from that creep. But he caught me one more time."

"Oh, my God. Your father would have killed him if he knew. Even if you didn't feel you could tell me, why not tell daddy? You were always closer to him."

"I think, not certain, for two reasons. I felt sorry for Aunt Lily for having such a disgusting husband, and knew about all her trouble with Brett. He had been left back. And I was too shy about sexual things at that age to tell dad."

Mom smeared her eye makeup while rubbing her eyes, which had filled with tears. Shaking her head, looking up at me, she asked, "Now what? What can I do to make it right so late?"

"Confront him. First tell Aunt Lily, shame him to the world. I want you to finally act like my mother! And this is not all about me. I'm sickened at the thought that he might touch Isabel someday. I will personally kill him if he lays a hand on my niece!" I became aware of other patrons looking at us after my outburst.

"Your aunt will be devastated. The thought of that conversation with her makes me ill. But I'll have it, you can be sure of that." Mom lapsed into a brief silence. Then, "He didn't rape you, did he?"

"No, but he did grab me again, years later, when I was outside and he came by to deliver new lawn furniture. No one else was home. You had taken Duchess to the groomer, and dad was away on business, as usual. Bob had rung the bell, but with no one answering, once he saw me, he knew I was alone, stretched out on a lounge in a bikini. He came up to me without a word, tried to kiss me, that disgusting lowlife. Probably would have raped me. I pushed him away. Spit in his face. Tried to kick him in the balls. Got him in the shin instead. He yelped. You know what that imbecile said? 'Why are you doing this?' I cursed him out, said I'd tell daddy and Aunt Lily. He started to cry, to crawl, begged my forgiveness, all to silence me. Of course I knew what he was doing. I screamed, 'Get out you fucking child molester. Don't ever come to this house again!' He ran out like an escaping prisoner."

In a quivering voice, my mother spoke: "Sally, you say you were fourteen. And a courageous kid you were. Why didn't you report that animal? He didn't deserve your protection."

"Don't even suggest that I protected him. I'm upset that you'd think that. I was sure daddy would kill him.

Then daddy would go to jail. What would happen to us? I let days, weeks pass. Afterward, if I heard Aunt Lily and that scum planned to come over, I stayed away. Of course, I couldn't avoid family events – like Brett's Bar Mitzvah. Remember how I refused to go up at the candle lighting ceremony when Bob was to hand me the candle? I took it from Brett."

"Your aunt was upset, yes, I remember. Now I feel so stupid. I yelled at you for making a scene. Where were my instincts? I can only defend myself by saying that in those days I never knew anyone to do such a thing. The idea that a Jewish man, a father, could molest a child, it was unthinkable. But of course, now all we hear about is that priests, rabbis, doctors, are convicted abusers. And we recently were treated to the spectacle of Judge Cavanaugh's confirmation hearings."

"What did you tell yourself about why your teenage daughter was promiscuous? You knew I was, right? I didn't have intercourse, but everything else was open season. Until now, this minute, I never made the connection between all the screaming you and daddy did about your lousy sex life, my seductive behavior with dad, Uncle fucking Bob, and my teenage generosity."

I felt closer to my mother than anytime in memory, relieved, admiring that she was able to listen. Now I'll have to see what she does with it. We headed to Bloomingdale's, splitting up, then agreed that I'd return to school, only seeing her in the morning for the airport run.

Traversing an emotional line from distrusting my

mother, to worrying about her, I paid attention to her at last. She seemed shrunken without the anger that once sustained her. Too sad, too guilty, even on the edge of too thin. Her last words to me that night: "Something vital has left me these past months. Is it energy? Or my always present irrational hope that my life with your father would magically improve? Now all I can hope for is that you and Larry and his family are well and happy. Nothing more for me."

We hugged at the airport with new affection mixed with a hint of sadness for all those lost years. Hope the transformation holds.

I'm grateful for work, able to lose myself no matter what else is happening around me. The Law Review article was challenging, citing current reports on legal representation of schizophrenics and other seriously mentally ill defendants. I attended all my classes, met regularly with my study group, at least two of whom were crazed about upcoming finals and fearing they'd fail their various states' bar exams. I loved working at the Legal Aid clinic where I was assigned mentally ill clients who needed patience and clear, unambiguous advice. Too bad I can't seem to give myself that.

It wasn't until I agreed to join my study group friends Monica and Shannon to celebrate their birthdays that this workaholic was willing to engage in anything social. The evening was enjoyable until they began comparing notes on their parents' plans for graduation weekend, months off. Shannon's dad, an oft-quoted surgeon who specializes in child facial reconstructive surgery, is hosting his large Irish family. Monica's parents, both from immigrant Greek families, their girl being the first to go to college, well, they are descending en masse. I tried a second mojito to distract me from my family's drama. But **WHERE IS MY FATHER?** replayed like an old broken phonograph record. **WHAT IF HE'S FINE BUT ELECTING TO REMAIN WHEREVER HE IS, WITH WHOMEVER HE'S CHOSEN?**

I jumped off the bar stool when Monica touched my shoulder. She had noticed my demeanor, asking, "What's with you? Are you bored with us?" How can I explain? These girls come from normal, loving families. If we're not close, it's because I've never shared personal stuff with them. And I won't start now. But I did apologize. "I'm exhausted. Rather than rain on your parade, I'm cutting out before falling asleep here. These drinks haven't helped."

Overriding their protests, I left, walking the twelve blocks to my place. I fell asleep quickly, only to be awakened around 2am with snippets of a dream, which I decided to record on my phone.

In the dream, daddy and I were on his boat, anchored at the pier on West 72nd Street. He's hugging me, saying how proud he is of me, and that he has bought me a new MAC laptop. Then he says that he's so sorry, he can't come to my middle school graduation. He has to take care of business and will be away that week. I struggle not to cry. I know that I can't get mad at him or he'll be angry and never come back. End of dream.

The rest of the night crawled on. No way could I sleep after such a dream. I did try to read in preparation for tomorrow's expert testimony class, but that was impossible. Television sometimes helped. Not this night. I watched an HBO Bill Maher rerun, hoping the country's political nightmare might distract me – or at least trigger laughter at the host's outrageous comments. At around 5 am, I succumbed. The alarm shocked me awake at 6:30. Like a dead one, I showered, dressed, grabbed a cold bagel from the fridge. Real life demanded priority.

On my way to work, Amy called. She claims she's worried about me. She is not the type of friend who asks if her advice is welcomed - so I should never, ever have confided my intention to take the Illinois Bar and possibly move in with Jonah. She's sure I don't love him. "So why run away from your future, a great career?"

Amy volunteers her opinion that Jonah is far from over the loss of his wife. "He just started to date, met you, and BOOM! That's insane. Both of you are escaping from your lives. Don't go there, friend." I was not gracious in terminating her lecture: "Enough, Amy... it's my life. See you tomorrow in class." And hung up.

My darling sister-in-law and my aunt were more circumspect. I certainly knew that neither thought much of what had begun as my and Jonah's fantasy - moving in with him - and had morphed into a plan. After sending that check in to register for the Illinois

Bar exam, I began shivering as if with a fever. Assuring myself that passing the exam would not require my move, should have worked. It didn't. Several troubling conversations with family and friends followed. I avoided sharing any specifics about my post-graduation plans, while they repeatedly shared theirs in minute detail.

CHAPTER 11

Within days of my mother's visit, Aunt Lily called. I had been dreading the confrontation. Should I have told mom, demanding that she tell my beloved aunt? Her message: "Call me whenever you are free to have a long, private conversation."

When I reached her, she initially sounded calm, inviting specifics. I needed her reassurance that she wasn't angry with me for telling my mother, and that she believed me. She understood that I expected her to confront her husband. Responding, "I'm devastated by what you went through. How I wish you had been able to out him at the time, with your parents and with me. I'm horrified by how alone you were, by your being injured by someone you should have been able to trust."

"So you're not angry – even with mom for deciding to tell you. How about my expecting you to do something, to confront your husband? I was afraid that you and mom would have a falling out, or that you might not believe me."

"That'd never happen! My initial reaction was to freak. Your mother and I spoke again right after I confronted Bob. I refused to let him off the hook. He acknowledged that he might have done what you described, though he claimed it happened once when he was drunk. He said he was ashamed. Not enough, by my sense. Right now I must figure out my life. How is it to discover that the man you've lived with for thirty years, once loved, the father of your child, is an evil stranger? A sexual deviant. After a brief silence, she added: "Your mother is going through a similar emotional shock over your dad's behavior."

"Please don't think you have to leave Uncle Bob for me. For all that I was shaken by his molesting me, I don't think it truly scarred me. If anything has influenced my relationships with men, it's my father's cheating and my parents' horrible relationship."

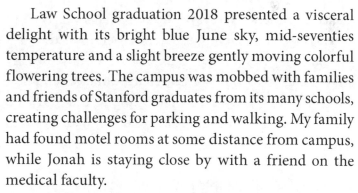

Law School graduation 2018 presented a visceral delight with its bright blue June sky, mid-seventies temperature and a slight breeze gently moving colorful flowering trees. The campus was mobbed with families and friends of Stanford graduates from its many schools, creating challenges for parking and walking. My family had found motel rooms at some distance from campus, while Jonah is staying close by with a friend on the medical faculty.

For all my relief at this beginning, any happiness I expected to feel was missing – dad's absence was so painful. Even graduating in the top ten percent of my class and with clinical honors did little to cheer me. My friends' warmth had an astonishingly contradictory impact. I cried - why hadn't I trusted them to be close?

A surprise was Carlos' visit just days before the big event, to wish me luck, gift me with a Mont Blanc pen (engraved Sally Marcus, Esq), and to offer me a job with his small, growing criminal defense firm. Turning him down, with pleasure I told him, exaggerating, that I am in a committed relationship with a cardiologist in Chicago. This newly minted JD is interviewing for an Illinois Supreme Court clerkship.

The evening prior to graduation, Jonah and my family met. I knew they'd love him – a Jewish doctor, and someone who loves family. Mom picked up the tab for a sumptuous seafood dinner after ascertaining that Jonah did not observe kosher dietary laws. And when Larry discovered that my boyfriend loves jazz, well, my brother was hooked. Aunt Lily showed intermittent staged liveliness. Naturally, no one made reference to Uncle Bob, who, of course, had not been invited.

Sadness overcame me as I said goodbye to my studymates. We would be scattered around the country, with only one, Leslie, also relocating to the midwest. She graduated with highest honors, and had accepted a faculty position at the University of Michigan, Ann Arbor.

These young people embraced their adult futures, while I knew myself to be an overage adolescent pretending to be an adult.

After seeing everyone off for home, depression hit me hard. Scary. Then my brother called – from the airport – and following a pretty strange beginning, launched into his big brother routine.

"Sis, we're all proud of you, but you know that already. Elisa thought I should keep quiet. That you're an adult, entitled – her word – to make your own decisions. Even if they suck!"

"Uh, oh…what are you getting at?" Guessing wasn't difficult.

"I – no, we – think your moving in with Jonah is way premature. There, I've said it!"

"I've heard that before from you. And maybe Amy talked to you? She sure hasn't pulled any punches in telling me what she thinks."

"Nope, no contact. How the devil would I talk to her – she's your friend. Mom is over the moon happy with Jonah. And we all like him. But – a big BUT – you two hardly know each other. Why not come back to New York? Or get a job in California; you love the weather, used to complain about New York winters. Chicago – you haven't known damp cold until you've lived there. Remember I survived the midwest for years."

"I know you want the best for me, but I have to make my own decisions. I do not want to return to New York. I do not want to stay here. I hate earthquakes, fires. Cold doesn't scare me. Jonah and I have talked about everything. We believe we're ready for the next step. Not marriage. But we need more time together, to be close, to develop our relationship. We care about each other, have similar values."

"I don't hear about love. About passion. How about renting your own place in Chicago once you get a job? I'll help with moolah. That makes more sense."

"Larry, darling, I do not have to put out my choices to have you, mom, even Elisa, make judgments about what's sensible for me. When I decided on Stanford, I stopped running my decisions past anyone. That works for me now as well."

"OK, sis… Elisa told me that you'd think I – we – were intruding. We both love you, and hope it works out. He's a decent guy. You're a great gal. Why shouldn't the two of you make it?"

Larry said goodbye, then added: "Come visit us soon, please. Our kids are growing up so fast…we want them to know their aunt."

After our call, I burst into tears yet again. Should I tell Jonah how prone to depression I am? He went through enough with his wife. Does he want to undertake a depressed girlfriend? Does he even know? Am I being a selfish bitch to put that on him?

I downed a sleeping pill. When I awakened the following morning, I did feel better. Not perfect. But okay. Bouncing back so fast allowed me to bypass any question of my disappointing a waiting Jonah.

Weeks after moving in with Jonah, notified that I passed my Bar exams, adjusting to my clerkship, I made what had been a long postponed decision – therapy. My unpredictable moods had continued in spite of my loving relationship with Jonah and having an interesting, if stressful job. I have no financial problems, am physically healthy, meeting new people, so why are some days so difficult to face?

David Held, M.D., had completed his residency at Michael Reese Hospital, after which he and a friend become partners in a psychiatric practice in a northern Chicago suburb.

The doctor's waiting room is nondescript except for two interesting water colors depicting happy young people on Telluride ski slopes. Dr. Held tells me, when I ask once in the inner sanctum, that he is a lifelong passionate skier, and had been on ski patrol in Breckenridge, Colorado during his years at the University in Boulder. His directness in responding to my questions warms me; I had one prior session with a female, analytically trained therapist whose every response to my inquiry was, 'What brings that question to mind?' I detested her.

Dr. Held and I got past the business concerning confidentiality and his fees, but had our first struggle when he suggested we meet twice a week. He didn't pursue this, instead encouraged me to use our time today.

"I've been a wreck on and off since graduation. No, even before that. Though my father's been gone for three years, I seem even more preoccupied with his absence now than before.

"When I'm up at 2, 3, in the morning, memories of when I was very little come rushing back. My dad's a blur. He came and went so often that it's almost impossible to connect him with everyday life. He generally tried to be with us for birthdays and graduations, and for summer weekends when we'd go out on his boat. We did vacation together, either on the boat or on driving trips through New England and Florida. I recall his frequent telephone calls when I was little, to wish me goodnight, to ask how a test or tennis match had gone, if I had found an outfit for my Bat Mitzvah." Without warning, I began to cry.

"His disappearance is a powerful loss, Sally. How surprising it would be if you didn't feel hurt, fear and perhaps anger. Do you typically discount your very natural emotions?"

We went on from there, with a tearful me making good use of his tissues, ashamed to be so out of control in front of a stranger.

"You look so unhappy, more about your tears than about what you're sharing. Tell me, Sally, were tears verboten in your family?"

So this is how it went, with David venturing connections between how I am and what I had shared of my history. He, asked very few questions about my current life. He seemed more interested in me than in the facts, so after our double session today, I began to feel a closeness to him, agreeing before I left to meet twice a week.

At our second appointment, I shared a dream from the previous night; I had slept well, drained from our first session. This dream started out like my repetitive childhood dream where the basement room goes on fire. What happened next is a bit blurry, but I know that my father was in it. He was around the age he is now, but I was a child – ten, perhaps – and just as I see him, he disappears into a vortex and vanishes. All I knew before awakening is that the child I was in that dream was terrified. Wanting to look, but too little to pursue him.

"What do you make of the dream, David?"

"You'd like me to associate to your dream, Sally? I could, because it's evocative, but it's your creation, so let's start with you."

"The first part is familiar. Now I know that the basement was scary because my rotten cousin Edwin used to take me there, saying he had something to show me, then hit me. Why I ever went back is a question. I should tell you - he died in a motorcycle accident five years ago, but not before terrorizing his retarded sister and causing a lot of pain to his parents."

David waited while I rambled on. I began to feel annoyed with him. "Are you the kind of analyst who doesn't say a word? I need more direction from you."

"So I've let you down already. I sense, Sally, that I have to be very supportive, very present, so unlike your father. But undoubtedly I will sometimes fail you. You might even experience me as failing when it's not quite how it is."

"You're referring to transference. I took psych courses at Barnard."

"Yes, you're on target there. We're all subject to experiencing that at times, especially when we need the person to be there for us - when we're vulnerable, as you are now."

"I shouldn't be vulnerable now. I have a great life!"

"It feels like we're arguing. Let me say that sometimes when we are at our happiest, if we have had substantial early losses, we're even more fearful of trusting the other person, of losing them. Might that be true for you?"

"Jonah says I sometimes act as if, to quote him, 'One wrong move and I'm dead.' He feels on shaky ground with me, and after I've been a bitch, I'm certain he'll leave me – by then sure I was terrible to him, I apologize. Sometimes he doesn't remember what I did to believe that."

"Has that been true of your other relationships with men?"

"Apart from my father? I've had so few relationships. My high school boyfriend was a keeper – both of us obsessed with tennis, academic nerds, very ambitious. He's enrolled in MIT for a doctorate in engineering. And, no, we didn't go through all this. But then again, we didn't have sex, had next to no arguments. I loved his parents. Visited with them some nights when Jimmy wasn't even there."

"And more recent relationships?"

"Only one. Carlos. We were like an intense flame that burns itself out. How's that for poetry? He and I are so alike – both complicated. I think I've had enough of this for today. Can we stop here?"

"Your choice, Sally. We still have time today. It could be helpful to stay, to give thought to why you suddenly feel you must leave."

"I've had enough for today. Don't I have the right to go as I please?"

"Of course, you do. We can pick up here next time."

Driving back to the office, I decided that I should - no, MUST, try to find my father. If it involves travel, I'll ask mom or Larry to finance it. Where to start was less clear. I opted to use my new leather-bound notebook to write down everything I knew so far. It wasn't much, but included where Dad had ever travelled for business or pleasure, people he knew there who might help, his language skills, his interests. And I labeled Chapter I: Dad's planned escape from his life - no criminal intent; Chapter II: Dad's plunging into criminal enterprise. Only after facing those two disparate possibilities could I be confident of my willingness to do the search.

I also decided that David was the right therapist for me.

CHAPTER 12

Jonah unexpectedly came home with a couple, Brian and Alan. Brian is a radiologist at Winnetka Radiological Associates; he and Alan, a hematologist involved in research and teaching, just returned from a six months' sabbatical in Bologna, Italy. Both had "insisted" on meeting me. So whispered Jonah, while opening wine. Jonah loves and admires them both, and they reciprocate. They brought Angel a colorful, crocheted bed, designed and made by their Italian host.

Tonight, waiting for delivery of Chinese food, Jonah and his pals caught up. I was beginning to feel irrelevant. Perhaps noticing, Brian turned to me: "We're so pleased for Jonah that you are in his life. We can see the difference in him." Naturally, after such a comment, I succumbed.

The guys and I talked while Jonah was setting the dining room table. Brian volunteered that he was devastated, standing by watching Jonah's wife, Anne, die such a horrible death: "The only saving grace was that it was swift, six months from diagnosis to the grave."

I wanted to hear more about Anne, about the couple's life together before the cancer. But they demurred: Alan volunteered, "It would be healthy for Jonah to be able to talk to you about all he's been through."

Neither man felt it was appropriate to divulge anything more. I understood why they might feel this way, but was disappointed, not yet ready to ask Jonah certain questions, the most important of which is, can he be truly emotionally free to invest in our relationship? Funny, I never asked myself that after Carlos.

Very different from my normal tentativeness with new people, I spontaneously hugged the men at the end of the evening.

We are happy, Jonah tells me. Some days I'm too self-involved to know what I feel. Can someone love and be loved and not be happy? On those days, I feel sure I'm crazy. Maybe I'm like my always-irritable mother. Naturally, every week I ask Dr. Held if it is inevitable for me to suffer from moods like my mother, and interrogate him as to his take on nature vs. nurture. But I also know that even a caring outsider cannot ask certain questions of us; we have to learn to ask them of ourselves.

Days after that visit, I seemed to have caught Jonah unawares when I asked him about his life before we met. Responding, "I thought I had told you," he at first appeared annoyed by my question. Then leading me into his study, he began a very emotional story.

"I told you that Anne and I went through medical school together. We were good friends. Both of us had other significant people in our lives 'til close to graduation. Anne was the warmest, most caring soul. When we were both single again, we became lovers, though I was never all that physically attracted to her. She wasn't what you call exciting, sexy. I felt tender, admiring, respectful. At times I imagined myself with another woman. She never knew. At least I hope that's true. I never, ever would have acted on my fantasies, but felt guilty at having them."

"I know you wouldn't have."

"Anne and I were beginning to talk about having children on our one year anniversary. We were close to the end of our residencies. She trained in hematology, I, in cardiology at a different hospital. She had selected her specialty in part because she wanted the option of working part-time when we had kids. I would be the primary breadwinner. So Anne went for a physical in anticipation of pregnancy. We were sure she was healthy, though she seemed exhausted from time to time." Jonah teared up, shook his head, silent. I reached for him, held him until he pulled away.

"I vividly remember that phone call on a Saturday in early November. We were lounging around, happy not having plans. In fact, Anne had asked me if I minded her canceling a midday date with friends. I was delighted. The call was from Dr. Rudin, who had completed his work-up and had just received the results. Anne's liver enzymes were off, so much so, he thought the test might have been messed up. But she and I immediately were concerned. Her occasional unexpected nausea, the minor appetite changes, small weight loss, recent fatigue – all of which we had previously ignored – took on more sinister meaning. By the end of the following week we got the diagnosis: end stage liver cancer."

"What a tragedy for such a young woman, and for you at the start of your lives together. Did she have family to help?"

"Yes, but not locally. She was from Montana, had younger twin brothers and an older sister. Her father had died young – of the same cancer. Her mother was – is – a wonderful woman. She stayed with us during the whole horrible ordeal. The chemo nearly killed Anne, leaving her desperately ill, so much so, she elected to stop it. I concurred. There was no point."

Jonah and I sat together in silence for a time. He seemed distant, remembering, while I tried to be patient. I finally asked him how it was for him afterward, who was there for him.

"Remember, I had just joined an existing practice, low man, so they drowned me in work, seven days a week, at times from 7am to near midnight. God knows how I didn't make any serious mistakes, walking around half dead myself. So, the work helped – for two years. By the time my friends were pushing me out, just months before I met you, I had become angry at the world. I felt my colleagues were taking advantage of me. Angry... guilty that I needed a woman in my life."

"Jonah, you're a healthy man, why guilty? Are you still? I mean, do you sometimes wish I wasn't around?" Thinking this, I felt an infusion of blood in my temples, the beginnings of a rare headache.

"Damn it, Sally. You wanted me to talk to you. I am, but now it's become about you. I do not feel guilty, haven't for months, even before meeting you. But do you want me to tell you what I do feel recently? I'm often frustrated with you. So many of our conversations focus on your obsessing about your father so that you aren't present with me."

Jonah had been so mild up until this evening that I was dumbstruck by his outburst. Worried, then relieved. Something I had sensed but never articulated had been under the surface had now emerged. Why is he attracted to me? Why does he want to push us forward, when we are so new together? I finally asked myself why I had jumped at moving to Chicago, to living with Jonah so soon after our Colorado meeting.

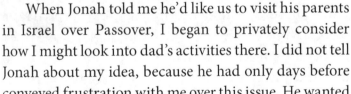

When Jonah told me he'd like us to visit his parents in Israel over Passover, I began to privately consider how I might look into dad's activities there. I did not tell Jonah about my idea, because he had only days before conveyed frustration with me over this issue. He wanted me to acknowledge that my dad had left the family and has stayed away because that's what he wanted to do. In inviting me to join him, Jonah mentioned that his parents were excited about our visiting, but also hadn't hid their concern at how soon after our meeting in Colorado we had begun living together.

I asked Jonah about his parents' relationship with

his late wife. He said they came to love each other, having spent time together on several occasions both in Chicago and in Israel. "Anne and my mom had a lot in common: science and loving me. Anne's being Protestant didn't matter a bit. My parents are secular Jews, like most Israelis." Jonah, his eyes filmed, continued: "Of course my parents stayed with me before and after Anne's funeral. They still keep in touch with her parents, and hosted her brothers on their trip to Israel last May."

Before leaving for Israel, Jonah and I visited my family in New York. Isabel, 4, is the family chatterbox, while her 1 ½ year-old brother Matthew entertains himself with matchbox cars, saying little. My brother seemed happy – able to quit his teaching job for full-time performances with his band. He's become locally famous as a jazz musician. We all went to dinner at Aunt Lily's – mom included – Uncle Bob out of the picture. My two mothers were gracious, but reserved.

Jonah slept on the interminable, packed El Al flight to Israel, as did many other, mostly Orthodox passengers. I had to stay awake to make sure the pilot was keeping the plane in the air. Following customs at Ben Gurion – me wiped-out - Jonah's dad met us. His mother, who teaches biology at Bar Ilan University, would join us later.

Benjamin Segal steered his 2014 navy Maxima with care during the short trip to Netanya, insisting that I sit beside him. We arrived at the family's tiny one-bedroom bungalow overlooking the beach; their main home is in Herzliya, where we will be spending most of our visit.

Mr. Segal, noticing my exhaustion, suggested that I take a nap on the sun porch. Later awakened by Jonah's boisterous reunion with his mother, I referenced my own mother's warning: "Make yourself presentable before meeting a boyfriend's family." But there's only one bathroom - I was nowhere near it – so I walked into the living room where the three were seated at a small formica dining table piled with snacks and soft drinks. I giggled to myself, recalling a Lucille Ball rerun where, to avoid detection, she crawled under and behind furniture to the bathroom, where she was outed, after dropping a heavy object on the tile floor. But as this wasn't television, I ventured forth.

Hugging me, saying "We're so happy to have you here," followed by "Naturally Jonah has talked about you on every call." His mom, undoubtedly noticing my predicament, suggested, "Perhaps you'd like to freshen up while we're preparing dinner." I could have kissed her.

Jonah's parents might be siblings; they are both slender, about 5'5", with graying dark hair and expressive eyes. His dad, near retirement from his aeronautical engineering job, sports a small mustache, which he touches often. His mom in a long black knitted skirt with a fitted white man's shirt, wears no make-up. Neither appears focused on personal appearance, and their small cottage is indifferently decorated, with comfort a priority. All in stark contrast to my family.

"Sally, please call me Rachel. Jonah said you've been to Israel before."

"Yes, many times, though not in recent years – for my brother's Bar Mitzvah, my Bat Mitzvah, volunteering with Betar, for Birthright, and as a Betar counselor, the summer following my freshman year at Barnard.

"You've waited too long to return. We'll just have to take you around, to see how much progress the country has achieved." Turning to her son, she adds, "That is, if you'd like us to join you both. Ben thinks I'm too pushy." She laughs as her husband nods. Jonah blows a kiss her way, and we all laugh. These are easy people to be with.

Later I watched Jonah sleep, on his stomach, arms over his head, pillows thrown on the floor. His parents had insisted we use their bedroom, while they are asleep on the sun porch. I found myself awake, so it's no surprise that I got to thinking back to my exciting last visit to Israel. On a kibbutz, my Betar group worked hard reorganizing a nearby battalion's warehouse. After two weeks, I had become ill with flu; dehydration led to a brief admission to Hadassah Hospital. On discharge, my dad arrived to take me to Tel Aviv to recuperate.

He and I spent several pleasant days at the Hilton, swimming, eating, sleeping, enjoying rare time in each other's exclusive company. But he had to complete work in Jerusalem. As I was still too weak to return to camp, he suggested that I invite my friend Ellie to accompany us there for a long weekend. We girls could hang around the King David Hotel pool. Dad would join us for dinners. He added an enticement: "The last time I stayed there, I saw at least twenty handsome young guys at the pool. Some great looking girls too. How I wished I was young again."

My memories had me smiling, relishing in our former closeness. That is, until that disturbing event resurfaced.

Dad, Ellie and I had been in the dining room at the hotel for our final dinner together before dad would be taking us back to camp. He was always a terrific storyteller. That night he shared an experience he had in Paloma during the running of the bulls, where he saw men trampled. While vividly recreating the event, dad was animated, relaxed, and we were attentive, though concerned, (as he was not), that we get back to camp on time. Then the atmosphere changed.

Ellie and I both turned to see what had captured my father's attention. Two short, slim young men, perhaps Arabs, were on the veranda, not quite hidden by tall bushes. They were motioning to dad. He rose, said he had to take care of something. Even now I have no clue why I did what I did next. Telling my friend that I wanted to secretly overhear their conversation as a joke, I saw her off to the bathroom. Then I sneaked outside, parking myself behind another tall bush as close as possible to where the three men were talking. Because they were whispering, I missed a lot of the conversation – but what I did hear, scared me. Dad said: "I'll get it for you, but it could be dangerous." One of the men whispered, angrily, "Don't use my name. We'll get you the cash." He handed my father something – what, I couldn't make out. I returned to our table, rejoining Ellie.

Once back at the kibbutz after Ellie left us, I asked dad who the men were he had been talking to. Responding with obvious irritation, he intoned: "It's not your concern. Go to bed!" before kissing me and leaving. Neither of us ever referred to the incident again.

With difficulty I returned to the present, determined to focus from my adult perspective on what I had witnessed. But sleep called before I came up with any reasonable interpretation.

My mother called this morning. She reported receiving a package, sent to me at Stanford, forwarded to Sea Cliff, before finally being delivered to her new address in Manhattan. It had a return address from a Barcelona boutique. Should she open it?

Imagining it might be from my father, I agreed. Inside the Hermes box was a gorgeous silk scarf in my favorite colors, cranberry and navy, the design depicting birds in flight. Mom texted me photos.

"It's from dad – I know it is. Did you find a card?"

Mom read a handwritten note: "This is from someone who loves you very much, is so proud of you at your graduation, and wishes you joy in your life. (No signature)

"It's definitely not your dad's handwriting. I want to believe he's alive, but it's hard after so long." Hesitating, she continued: "If he's alive, he's up to no good. How is it possible that a man who was so devoted to Israel, to Jewish causes, might have done something against them?"

"Mom, don't jump to conclusions. Maybe he was acting as an undercover peace envoy – that could explain his trips to those other countries." (Anxious to hold my present, close to tears, I silently thanked God to learn that dad was alive and thinking of me.)

"You want to believe your father's innocent? I talked to your Uncle Philip last month. We spoke of nothing else. He volunteered that dad needed money, and likely undertook god knows what to get it. How is that possible, when we had millions? Did he owe money to someone? When I asked for specifics, Philip denied knowing anything. He told me that when he last saw Sam, he felt it was a goodbye visit."

"He never told me that! I always loved Uncle Philip. But I wouldn't necessarily trust his word or his judgment."

"He swears that being in prison had given him time to think. That before his plea deal, he was obsessed with what could happen to him, and had little interest in our dilemma. That's believable."

We were invited to first Seder with Jonah's extended family. His aunt Louise is the family hostess and chef; others bring special Passover items like macaroons and kosher wine. The celebration took place in Louise and Abe's apartment just blocks from the Segal's. I was amazed that 23 people can be hosted in such a small space. Though most speak English, Hebrew dominated conversation, with everyone speaking at once before and after the Seder. Jonah translated. In addition to ritual reading of the Haggadah in which we all participated, we sang, led impressively by Uncle Abe. The children, ages 7-16, were given diluted wine. Seven year old Alana asked the questions. Naturally at the end of the Seder, she found the afikoman and collected $5. I was relieved that no one made much of a fuss about me, or asked me uncomfortable questions, except as we were leaving, when Aunt Louise asked Jonah when we will get engaged. This family is used to visitors from the states, no big deal. Overall, a fun evening, which ended with all of us pitching in for the clean-up.

Over breakfast, Jonah's parents treated me to their perspective on "…what's really going on in Israel." His mom is frustrated by many U.S. colleges dumping Israeli bonds. "… they see us as the perpetrators, the Palestinians as being victimized. The fact that Hamas is intent on our destruction, that they commit terrorist attacks whenever possible – liberal Americans ignore that particular reality." His dad had distrusted Obama: "He was too clever to openly abandon Israel, but he did not have our back!" I defended our former President, reminding them that a two-state solution was fast becoming impossible with all the expanded settlements. Both parents shocked me with their trust in Trump, though they recognize his obvious flaws. And they support Bibi Netanyahu. What a team these two leaders make. I shut up, helped by Jonah reminding me - as if I didn't already know - that we in the U.S cannot relate to the vulnerability Israelis have as a tiny country in the midst of hostile states. The long war in Syria had temporarily reduced some of those states' focus on Israel, and increased bipartisan trade with the Gulf states, as well as joint efforts on desalination and the development of natural gas reserves with Jordan.

Jonah is so different around his parents. With friends and colleagues, he is warm and engaging, but from my vantage point, a bit constrained, not always saying what he truly believes. Here, he is completely himself, able to be quiet if he chooses, to disagree with his dad or kibitz with his mom. The three of them obviously are certain of their love for each other. Remembering my own contentious adolescence, I asked Jonah how he and his parents managed in his teens. He swears he never had a serious argument with either parent until, after graduating from Yale, he informed his parents of his intention to remain in the states for medical school. His dad blew up, then disappeared for hours, only to apologize, reassuring Jonah that as a man he had the right to decide what was best for himself.

I was ashamed of my jealousy, not of Jonah's love for them, but of their unconditional love for each other. Wanting to be inside that circle, I became conscious that something keeps me apart. One crazy thought is that Rachel will see me as damaged, and confide this belief to her son. Or that shocking news about my father will surface; afterward Jonah's parents will believe I've been tainted by dad's crimes. God forbid, what if my father betrayed Israel? These patriots would then have sound reason to distrust me. I struggled to pull myself out of this obsessive ditch. The words faded, but not so much the underlying feelings.

I had planned to spend two full days away from the Segals to see what I might learn about my dad's activities in Israel. Jonah made it right with his parents, who, I'm sure, were happy to have some alone time with their son. I decided on taking the bus from Tel Aviv to Jerusalem, overcoming his parents' objections – they had wanted to drive me.

Before leaving, I tried to reach Larry, but ended up speaking to Elisa. How remarkable that, for the first time ever, after my telling her about my plans here, she shared her still powerful pain over the loss of her parents.

"Every year as mothers' and fathers' days approach, I feel sick. I look at my kids. How much they would have been loved. My mom was crazy about children. Did you know she had been a kindergarten teacher until retirement five years before their deaths? Daddy was a bit less comfortable around kids - at least 'til they were school age. Then he loved playing ball with them. And Larry - they made him their son. Has he ever spoken to you about how devastated he was at their deaths?"

I listened in silence until bursting: "You mean so much to me, Lissy. I'm grateful that you have finally been able to share. It's so often about me, the kids, Larry, when we speak."

After a moment, she said that our family's craziness had made it so difficult for her to pay attention to herself. "Now that Larry is okay, and your mom seems more together, I guess I've given myself permission to feel again."

We spent the remainder of our Whatsapp conversation on girl talk: Elisa wanted to know more about Jonah and me, his parents and me, etc., only then shifting to volunteer that she was just elected President of her kids' PTA, and is also learning bridge.

After our goodbyes, I was again left with the contrast in our lives: hers was so normal, mine so uncertain.

CHAPTER 13

While registering at the King David Hotel, I watched an English language news program detailing still another United Nations' effort to resolve differences between Gaza and the Palestinian government on the west bank. But threats from Gaza toward Israel intensify, supported by Iran's Hamas, prompted by Israel's destruction of tunnels from Gaza, which the enemy had used to infiltrate the country. Iran, its troops so close to Israel, is actively assisting Syria's murderous leader, and openly conveys its intent to see Israel destroyed, even in the midst of their own country's economic devastation due to our sanctions. The hotel clerk remarked: "We'll be at war again, of that you can be sure." An older employee called him away, no doubt to lecture his underling against scaring tourists.

I am past listening to those who have advised me to come to terms with dad's disappearance, to move on. I found support from my mother, whose final words during that telephone call were, "You owe it to yourself to do everything you can to find out where he is, and how he is." And Jonah helps: "Follow your own instincts, Sally. Don't let fear deter you." But I know he still resents my uneven availability to him.

The King David Hotel manager I once consulted,

still employed here, was generous in response to my request for information. Months ago, he had given me the dates of dad's last stay here. Today, I needed more: the names of dad's friends, and how I might contact them. Though reluctant, concerned that he could get in trouble, he provided me with three names after I conveyed just how worried my mother and I were about dad's disappearance. I promised eternal secrecy to protect him.

Sweating and shaky, I placed the first call to Matti Stein. A woman who identified herself as his wife, Gila, answered. She took my information, in Hebrew, responding in English: "My husband is not at home and would not appreciate my giving you his phone number!"

I ventured out onto the veranda, sipping coffee, looking over the pool to the very spot where dad and those men had spoken in a clandestine manner so many years ago. Making notes, chewing cinnamon Altoids – my mouth on fire – I heard my name on the loudspeaker: "Calling Miss Sally Marcus. Please come to the lobby for a call."

Matti Stein was a lot friendlier to me than was his wife, for whom he apologized. "She doesn't know your father. He was my business friend. Besides, I'm afraid Gila is suspicious by nature. Please, as Sam's daughter you are welcome to visit me in my office."

The Steins live in Beersheba in a spacious old stone house, likely once owned by a wealthy Arab family. The office is in a newer, two room building on the property. A short, balding, sixtyish man sporting Levis loosely belted below his protruding belly, welcomed me. His immediate query: "What can I tell you about your daddy? I consider him my friend. But I haven't seen him in more than a year. Closer to two."

Shocked and excited at his statement, I asked Mr. Stein to tell me what he recalled about that meeting, after sharing my family's distress at dad's disappearance.

"Well, young lady, your daddy and I did business together. He is likely just fine, but busy… What do you know of his work here?" He waited for my reply, while I pondered how I might word this so as not to put him on guard.

"I knew he was bringing machinery to Israel. No specifics. He was pretty secretive with me and with my mother. He spoke more openly with his brother, of course." I wanted this man to think that dad wasn't hiding from all of us.

"Okay. We're both on the same side, yes? Your daddy wanted to help Israel. He understood that some restrictions your government placed on what the U.S. would sell us were unfair. They give us plenty, more under Trump. In return your government thinks we should do what they want. That's not always our way. Sometimes… At any rate, the politics here are complicated. Israel can't be seen to flout your country's laws. So your daddy, he and I found other ways."

"Wouldn't you both be in danger if you got caught?"

"Maybe. You shouldn't be naïve, though. If our government needs something, even if they got wind of what we were up to, well, they just might look away."

"But then how could what you obtained be used, if illegal?"

"Look, young lady, the contraband is not an airplane or a ship. It's software, electronic parts for guidance. Small stuff. Precious to us. And some of those items became legal years after we imported them."

"Is there any chance dad would have helped other countries in the region? Like Egypt, Jordan, Kuwait?"

Matti Stein's face shifted to resemble a man having a stroke. Enraged, he shouted, "Absolutely not. This meeting is over." He pushed me – no, shoved me, into the courtyard. As a last effort, I attempted to thank him, but he had already slammed the office door shut.

In the taxi on the return trip, I had to fight off self-disgust at my handling of the interview, and a fleeting impulse to end the whole investigation. But once back at the hotel, I made extensive notes before treating myself to a refreshing nap; afterward, I ventured alone into the dining room with Hillary Clinton's "What Happened?." Consuming two fantastic salads, one chopped vegetables, the other fresh fruit topped with sherbert, with matzo, of course, I felt proud of myself for conquering my chronic discomfort at eating alone in a fancy dining room. Until recently, I would have ordered room service.

As I awaited the check, my cell phone rang. Heads turned, no doubt annoyed. The number was blocked. In the states I would never have answered.

"Am I talking to Sally Marcus?" When I responded in the affirmative, a woman who identified herself only as Matti Stein's niece, said she wanted to talk to me and I should come to see her in Ashkelon. In heavily accented English, she gave me directions, and ordered me to "Be here by 7 am sharp!" I agreed. She hung up.

Thank goodness for concierges. She had me safely ensconced in an air-conditioned Mercedes taxi and on my way by 6am, coffee in hand. Having been awake most of the night, I had made good use of the time, typing a list of potential questions I hoped this woman could answer.

Miri was just where she said she'd be, in front of a modest two-story whitewashed condo. From the car, I noted a few buildings showing damaged stone facades. Colorful wild delphiniums, wisteria and hydrangeas softened the image. My driver, a former Israeli colonel, volunteered that the damage had been the result of rockets from Gaza, years before, though "...largely ineffective because thank God they have no guidance system for accuracy."

Miri appears to be about my age, petite, with long dark hair sporting home applied blond streaks. She physically pulled me into her apartment, which would be called a studio in the states. She then watched through the Pullman kitchen window to make certain my driver had left, as per her orders. It was too warm in the small space, in spite of two tiny working fans on what had been a cool April morning.

Miri instructed me to sit facing her, with me on the two-seater couch upholstered in a harsh beige nubby fabric, she on a beat-up maple rocking chair. Her constant rocking distracted and unnerved me, as did her staring at me in silence. When I couldn't tolerate it any longer, I babbled: "Miri, I so appreciate your seeing me, especially now with all that you may have heard from your uncle about my meeting with him. I have concerns, questions, about my father. I'd be grateful for any help you can provide. And please, thank your Uncle Matti."

"Speak Hebrew! You're Jewish, aren't you? Didn't you learn it at school?" After that command, she in fact switched to Hebrew. I was in trouble here. Yes, I can read and write some, but a fluent speaker, I'm not. So I implored her, in my fractured Hebrew, to speak slowly.

"I am your sister. Your father is my father. He loved my mother and they made me out of love. Did you know that?"

Covering my mouth for fear I'd scream and surely regret it, I just shook my head. "No, I know nothing. How old are you?"

"Twenty-five, like you. Our mothers were pregnant the exact time, but you came first by a little."

We spent the next hour comparing notes on our lives, or at least, she asked me questions and I answered them. Occasionally, she responded to my question or volunteered something. She, like Matti Stein, had seen our father for the last time approximately 1 ½ years ago. He had come for a visit to her mother and Miri, leaving her $1500. How like him. He told her he needed to cut short the visit because of business, and promised to see her again soon after. Subsequently he sent her one notecard from London. There has been no further contact.

At this, Miri leaped up, reached high into her hall closet, accessing a large rectangular plastic box filled to the brim with photos and notes from dad. Smiling at me with warmth not previously in evidence, Miri invited me – in fluent English – to look over everything in the box. She was delighted to have me in audience; I could not refuse.

Later, Miri expressed disappointment when I turned down her invitation to stay the night. She had to leave early to volunteer in a nearby nursing home because of staff shortages over the Passover holiday. Before I left, promising I'd keep in touch, Miri called her mom, whom she addressed as Batya, and then wrote names of two men with whom our father had conducted business in Israel.

Jonah, hours later, had to listen to my near hysterical recital of the day's events. Initially he was sympathetic, but shifted to urging me to rethink my investigation. "Now that you know that your dad is alive and away by choice, why not return to my parents' home for the balance of our time here?" Rejecting that, irritated, I said a hasty goodnight.

But sleep was hard to come by after this remarkable day. I obsessed over how to tell mom about Miri's existence. How will Larry react? He already detests our father. And Miri wants to meet my family; she hopes to have me meet her mom and the rest of that family.

Should I agree? I believe my mother would be hurt should I embrace Batya.

Turning on the light, I eyeballed two names given to me by Miri's mother, whom Miri called my father's "true love." The first name jumps out at me: Ben Fisher. I went to camp with his daughter, Jamie, then caught up with her during freshman orientation at Barnard. I remember that her father and mine had business dealings. The two men acted like buddies when our parents showed up at Camp Ramah when we were both 12. They had wandered off by themselves while our mothers chatted. Fast forward, in our senior year at Barnard, Jamie told me that her mom had died of breast cancer, and her dad had sold their Long Island house, headed for Boca Raton. But now he apparently lives in Israel – in Tel Aviv. Having known him, it will be easiest for me to call Mr. Fisher.

A troubling scene from my high school years unexpectedly popped up. My boyfriend and I had been stretched out on the den couch following a basketball game, 'making out,' my shirt and bra off, his penis hard at my side. Dad entered the darkened room, heading for his desk.

Dad had placed a long-distance call without turning on the desk light, which even then I thought odd. He reached a man he called Benny, and after pleasantries, in a low-pitched voice proceeded to talk business. From what I could hear from dad's side of the conversation, his friend must have disagreed with dad's wish to expand their business to other countries. I recall only one of my father's statements in full – one that scared me: "We could be in enough trouble already, so why stop now?" The man at the other end of the call must have been Ben Fisher.

I will meet up with Jonah later today, then spend our last evening in Israel in Netanya. But before arranging my taxi this morning, I called Mr. Fisher; he took his time answering the house phone.

"Yes, of course I remember you, Sally. You and my daughter were good friends. How is your mother?"

I thought it telling that he didn't include my father, but decided against following up for now. Instead, without specifying the reason behind my call, I asked if my fiance and I could pay him a visit later this afternoon. Though it is likely he was surprised, he did not then inquire as to why I wanted to see him.

Jonah was not happy to spend his last afternoon in Israel "...on a wild goose chase." But I begged him to join me, and he didn't refuse.

Ben Fisher at 60 is a distinctive looking man, 6'3", slim, and youthful-appearing, with a full head of reddish blond hair and rich mustache. Living alone in a pleasant Tel Aviv condo, its small terrace overlooking an artificial pond, our host at first glance seemed content. We were treated to too-sweet iced tea and oreo cookies before Mr. Fisher, after some hesitation, inquired as to the reason for our visit.

Jonah responded by thanking him for his hospitality, at which point, sweating, I began: "I need help in finding my dad; he left us over three years ago to travel here on business. We haven't heard a word since." (leaving out the scarf present) "Naturally we are very concerned. His firm's spokesperson indicated that dad's last Israel trip was not for their company, as dad had retired shortly before leaving New York. Please – I beg you – please tell me whatever you can."

Mr. Fisher asked, "Why me?" I felt my anger rising, reluctant to respond. He continued: "You won't go to the Israeli police, I assume. You understand? He would be labeled a smuggler here as well as a traitor to his own country. He and I did some business together before I moved to Israel. He continued without me, but last we talked – maybe two years ago - Sam said he was through. It had become too dangerous. Where he is now, I have no clue."

Tears had been pooling on my cheeks. A likely startled Ben Fisher looked to Jonah to rescue the situation as I made a precipitous exit for the bathroom. On my return, the two men were engaged in quiet conversation about real estate in Tel Aviv.

"Can you even make an educated guess as to where my dad might be?"

"He liked London. Also Barcelona. For a while he lived in both places. He had remarried. The woman was English. She had a fancy dress shop in London. They traveled together. Maybe she had retired. I met her here on Sam's last visit. She's good-looking, smart, around 50 years old. Name's Alice something. That's all I know."

Jonah and I looked at each other before I spoke again. "Dad never divorced my mother. So how could he remarry?"

Ben chuckled. "You're kidding yourself, young lady. Your father never obeyed rules he didn't like. What, with all he did, you think he'd worry about a little bigamy?"

"You dislike him, don't you? How could you have done business with him for so many years, not having respected him?"

"I was always a devoted family man. You may laugh at me, a thief, a so-called enemy of my country. But I never cheated on my wife. I have standards; he never did."

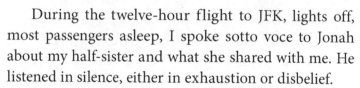

During the twelve-hour flight to JFK, lights off, most passengers asleep, I spoke sotto voce to Jonah about my half-sister and what she shared with me. He listened in silence, either in exhaustion or disbelief.

"Dad met Batya while she was a graduate mechanical engineering student at Cooper Union and he was an adjunct in business practices there. From friendship, they fell in love. When Batya got her degree, without a job and with her student visa about to expire, she returned to Israel. Unbeknownst to her, she was pregnant. Though dad sent money to support the child, he showed no interest in visiting Batya or in meeting his daughter. He finally met them when our family was on Larry's Bar Mitzvah trip. Can you imagine?"

"Yeah. He had quite a mess to deal with. According to you, your father solved most of his problems with money. Many men would have walked away, so at least he was financially responsible. Committed relationships were not his strong suit."

"God, Jonah, you're generous to a man who probably doesn't deserve it. You have such a normal family. Have you ever considered what you've gotten yourself into by taking me on?"

"What does your father's behavior have to do with you? If I had reason to distrust you, you'd be history." Jonah looked away; then, taking a deep breath while grabbing my hand, asked: "How about we get engaged? Whadda do you think?"

"In the middle of this mess, how can you expect that of me? I do care for you, Jonah. Please let me finish this journey before we..." Not allowing Jonah's non-verbal irritation deter me, I continued: "It must have taken some doing for my father to sneak away to see Batya and Miri on that ten day trip before Larry's Bar Mitzvah. Our family had been travelling with two other families and our Rabbi. We went everywhere together. When did dad find the opening to see them? Did I tell you that Miri had dad's picture from that meeting – she was seven years old - on her bulletin board. Plus she kept every note he ever sent her. Batya had married when Miri was two years-old, so the child had an on-site daddy. But she romanticized our father. Just like me, huh?

"Over the next ten years, dad paid unexpected visits to Israel during which he saw Miri. She was thrilled when for her high school graduation, dad treated her to an Italy trip, meeting her in Rome for a long weekend. How in hell did he pull that off? Mom must have bought into his lie about his taking still another business trip."

"Your mom wanted to believe him. Otherwise she would have been forced to break up the family. Was that trip around the time you started Barnard?"

"No. Miri is two years behind me in school. She's younger by five months. I skipped a grade, so it would have been the summer before my junior year. And Miri went into the Israeli army before college. She completed her degree last June and began teaching in September."

Jonah and I, covered with tiny, ineffective blankets, huddled for warmth. He slept. I didn't, sensing his hurt, his disappointment.

At some point, clear that sleep wouldn't come, I strained to recapture events during Larry's Bar Mitzvah trip. Stupid memories emerged – like another father on the trip giving me pomegranate, which I spit out, shaming my parents. Then there was that bomb scare in Jerusalem, while mom and I were in front of a jewelry store. Mom had refused to move, telling me that "New Yorkers are not cowards – we can handle this." Dad, elsewhere during the incident, joked with the other men over dinner: "You think a bomb scare can interfere with my wife's shopping?" I couldn't recall a time when dad left us during that trip.

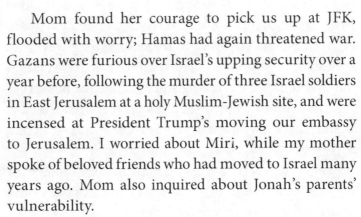

Mom found her courage to pick us up at JFK, flooded with worry; Hamas had again threatened war. Gazans were furious over Israel's upping security over a year before, following the murder of three Israel soldiers in East Jerusalem at a holy Muslim-Jewish site, and were incensed at President Trump's moving our embassy to Jerusalem. I worried about Miri, while my mother spoke of beloved friends who had moved to Israel many years ago. Mom also inquired about Jonah's parents' vulnerability.

Once in mom's condo, I was able to sleep at last. On awakening, I overheard Jonah and my mother on the tail end of their first extended private conversation, which surely he had initiated.

"Rhoda, I'm worried about Sally. Not because she's searching for her dad. I think she's depressed – stuck – whether it's about us, or about her work. She hasn't made friends in Chicago, repeatedly claims she can't concentrate at work. She believes she could be fired."

"Impossible. Sally was always the most responsible, at school, on jobs, even as a fifteen year old babysitter. Are you sure?"

"It's not that she's irresponsible. She uses the word 'disengaged."

"Jonah, I know that Sally is afraid of what she'll find out about Sam. My therapist says that when I gave up denying that Sam was unfaithful, then didn't asked about his trips to places he had no reason to visit, I was flooded with memories, with anger, with guilt. Maye that's what's happening to Sally now. I got past it; she will too. Don't worry so much. But don't expect too much of her now. She'll come around."

"I hope so. Sally told me about her Uncle Bob. It kills me that he can't be prosecuted because of that damned statute of limitations. Those laws should be changed!".

"I agree. But Bob has been punished. He lost his marriage and his son. He had to leave New York, lives in Florida with his brother. They detest each other; so Bob has a lifetime sentence." Rhoda chuckled at the thought.

In reporting the telephone conversation he had with his dad, Jonah told us that his parents brought their gas masks to a central station to have them checked out. This news – shocking to me – Jonah treated as commonplace. I reminded my mom of her response to that long ago bomb scare. Now she admits her behavior was "…nuts! If I hadn't been afraid for myself, why wasn't I more protective of you?" Good question.

I had asked Jonah to get lost for a couple of hours so that I might have a private, very difficult conversation with my mother about Miri.

"Mom, the Israel trip was extraordinary in so many ways. I already told you about the people dad worked with, and about Jonah's loving family. But I left out the most important stuff."

Mom's face betrayed her shift from curious to anxious when she began biting her lower lip. I continued. "Dad has a daughter in Israel, five months my junior. Her name is Miri. Dad supported her, kept in touch with her and with her mother – not romantically – until two years ago."

I shut up long enough to embrace my tearful mother before continuing. She reassured me: "Why should I be shocked? Why should I give a shit what he did?" But she struggled to stop crying, belying her words.

"Do you want to know anything more, Mom? I haven't yet told Larry. But I need you both to know that I intend to keep in touch with Miri. She was so happy to meet me, wants to be a part of my life – of our lives."

"Sally, you're an adult. Feel free to make your own decisions. I'm not angry and I will not tell you what to do. I thought I had known all the sordid details about your father's life. Now here's another one."

"We all better steel ourselves for what we'll learn if and when daddy surfaces. We think we're prepared. But the reality may be much worse."

I withdrew into the guest bedroom to place a call to Miri. We briefly spoke of what's happening in her town. Then, reassuring her that I want us to have a relationship, I told Miri that my mother now knows about her, but is not ready to meet her. The usually loquacious Miri was silent. I could hear her choking back sobs.

Afterward, I called my brother and Elisa. From Larry, "Why should I give a shit?" Elisa just listened.

Nothing about her father-in-law's behavior seems to shock her at this juncture.

Elisa shared something more important to her. Duchess had to be put down. This was the children's first encounter with death. They were both despondent. Matthew had asked for a puppy but Larry and Elisa rejected that for now. We agreed that a replacement is not the answer. Though I had been away from Duchess for years, and this loss was not unexpected, I too felt her death – she was my childhood best friend. Larry had decided to bury her in a pet cemetery on Long Island - at Bide-a-Wee. He demanded that I attend a memorial service for her: "Our kids need that. Mom agreed to come. So get your ass here, kid!"

Of course I would attend, though, to be honest, the whole idea of a pet memorial service seemed weird and expensive. Larry will pay.

Jonah seemed unhappy with me staying in New York, but tried, I believe, to hide his frustration. After I explained how as a child I slept with Duchess, how I talked to her by the hour, sharing all my hurts and fears, he was sympathetic, saying that his dog helped him survive his wife's terminal illness and afterward, her death.

What I learned about Jonah during this interchange - something I hadn't fully understood before - was that he is the quintessential scientist, practical, fact-driven, not hard-wired to make emotion-based decisions. And he hates emotional scenes. Boy, are we different!

The balance of my New York visit was spent with

family, including an afternoon at the pet cemetery. It turned out to be a bonding experience with my nephew. Until then, Matthew hadn't connected with me, nor I with him. But on that day, he held my hand, and spoke more than usual. "Tell me about Duchess when you were my age, Aunt Sally." I did, and silenced Isabel when she was tempted to interrupt him.

CHAPTER 14

The manager of the elegant Hermes shop in Barcelona spoke excellent French accented English.

"Madame, I was not at home when this beautiful scarf, purchased in your shop, arrived. Unfortunately, my mother accidentally threw out the gift card, so I have no way of knowing who sent it. But mother recalled it was from a woman. For such an elegant gift, I must send an appropriate thank you."

After a short interruption during which she accessed her computer files, Mme Rosario returned. "We had five buyers of this particular scarf during the period of time it was purchased. It is a very popular item in Spain, because that particular bird is believed to bring us good luck."

Of the five purchasers, two were women, both requesting gift wrapping, and one was mailed to New York. I was able to convince her to give me information about that buyer.

Alice Leland answered the telephone by identifying herself by name. I was extremely nervous. It seemed possible that I could soon hear about my father. Before calling, I had been practicing the conversation, trying out two versions. In one, I said, I'm Sally Marcus; in the second, I pretended that I was calling from the

Barcelona shop. Realizing that both my Spanish and French were marginal, I dropped the subterfuge.

"Mrs. Leland, ny name is Sally Marcus. Please don't hang up. I'm calling to thank you for the beautiful scarf. On my recent return home from a trip, I found the gift."

"Ms. Marcus, I purchased the scarf on behalf of a customer who prefers anonymity. Thus I am not free to disclose the individual's name."

"I'm certain we both know who it is. My father, Sam Marcus. I beg you to let me know how I might contact him. Or if you choose not to do that, give him my number. I live in Chicago now. Dad and I have lost touch for a few years, which you undoubtedly know. Please tell him that I will be getting married soon and would be devastated if he wasn't there to give me away."

"You may leave your number with me, Miss Marcus. I cannot confirm who the purchaser was. I am not even sure myself, and will have to consult my records. You have reached a gift shop in London. Many of our customers use our services to purchase items we do not carry."

Now I was confused. Is it possible that Alice Leland is not my father's so-called 'wife', but only the shop's manager?

When I hadn't heard from Mrs. Leland for several days during which time I was near worthless at work, I began obsessing about next steps. Then Jonah came up with a brilliant idea. Why not ask his friend from medical school, who lives and works just outside London, to go by the shop and take a gander at this lady? Since we have a good description of her from Ben Stein, it would be a slam-dunk to confirm or rule out her identify. The decision made, Jonah exercised his offer a-sap.

About 1 am, Mitch called. Alice Leland perfectly matched Ben Stein's description. She had to be dad's 'wife.' What's more, Mitch had gotten her home phone from the London telephone directory. Jonah, who had an extended conversation with his old buddy, told me Mitch was having a ball playing sleuth.

Ms. Leland initiated contact, calling me from her home. "I feel so foolish that I never considered the possibility that you would locate me. Sam did ask me to mail the gift for your graduation, and dictated the card. I'm pleased that you like the scarf. He informed me of your favorite colors. On vacations I have visited that Barcelona shop to select items for customers. I ordered your gift online, writing your father's loving sentiments. Since you called, I have been trying, without success, to contact him."

Shocking myself by my response, I asked, "Why should I believe that?"

"Please, I appreciate how distressed you are and have been during your father's absence, how much you want to reconcile with him. I give you my word that I will pursue the issue. But keep in mind that Sam often doesn't contact me for weeks, even months. He will, eventually; of that, I'm confident."

Hanging up, I burst into tears. I woke Jonah. He tried to comfort me, but to no avail. When I said that I am considering going to London, he chastised me: "You are not thinking clearly, Sally. You'll lose your job, and for what? Your father might be anywhere. If this Leland woman can be trusted, and it seems she can be, she will give him your message whenever he contacts her."

"How can I be assured that she can be trusted? I'm a mess. It's impossible for me to concentrate at work. It wouldn't surprise me if I were fired."

"Guess what, young lady? I demand that you pull yourself together. The woman I love, respect, hope to marry someday, won't let herself fall apart. You're so close to finding your father. Hang in there."

He then seduced me. It was the best night's sleep I had in weeks.

I woke up this morning having had a weird dream. It seems that in it, I am a presence in an unspecified large, black space. Is it me? The observer is not defined, even as to gender. Suddenly, in newly brilliant, flashing light, hundreds of enormous black cockroaches are seen fleeing, headed for what might be an exit. The observer does not react to the scene, seems without curiosity, to feel nothing. Dream over. On awakening, I have no difficulty interpreting the dream sequence. And this without needing Dr. Held encouraging me to associate.

The dream reflected my awareness that in the process of my shedding light on dad's disappearance, I am likely to find disgusting truths. The observer in the dream did not flinch from the ugliness. She – I assume it was a female – me - watched calmly, almost scientifically, intent on knowing. The genderlessness must mean that I must adopt that attitude, and not hide behind my femaleness, associated with fragility.

I reassured myself that whatever I will learn can't possibly be worse than what I imagine. Then, out loud, I contradicted that notion: you will be horrified and better be prepared.

CHAPTER 15

Jonah and I had hardly seen each other since our return to Chicago following our Israel trip. He was scheduled for a month's evening hospital duty for the practice, while I work days.

My office receptionist, Roberta, rang me the first Wednesday after our return. Working on neglected research, I had not scheduled any appointments, and may have sounded annoyed at the interruption. Roberta whispered: "I don't think you can avoid seeing this one."

Robin McMahon had identified himself as FBI. Sweating profusely, my legs shaking, my heart beating unnaturally fast, I opened my office door to admit the man. He must have spoken – I did see his lips moving – but he lapsed into silence until I finally responded: "I don't believe any of the Judge's cases have potential FBI involvement."

Mr. McMahon, his hand on my back, led me to the sofa, then power-opened a window. The soft breeze was refreshing.

"Ms. Marcus, we know you have been trying to locate your father. We are also interested in talking to him, and thought you might be open to helping us." Watchful, the agent waited for my guarded response.

"How do you know? Why? I mean, why do you want to talk to him? About what?"

"Please don't play dumb. I'll be direct with you. We have for some time been keeping track of Mr. Stein's calls, as well as Ms. Leland's. Mr. Stein is cooperative, for his own personal reasons. Not so Ms. Leland. Until now, she claimed to know nothing about your father's whereabouts, insisting that they have been out of contact for two years. She told you a very different story. We do not appreciate being lied to. As you are an attorney, I am sure you are fully able to grasp the implications of covering for a fugitive, even if he is your father."

"I hate that word. He's never been convicted of anything, has he? Look, I must consult my own attorney. I don't have anything to hide from you; as of now I know nothing!"

Mr. McMahon left, his card prominently displayed on my desk. His last words: "We'll meet again very soon." I collapsed in fright, an incipient migraine precluding further work today. Leaving the office, I tried unsuccessfully to reach Jonah from a nearby coffee shop, but did not leave a message. On the bus ride to the apartment, I reassured myself: I hadn't done anything wrong. But I also could imagine that my sixty year-old father might live out his life in a federal penitentiary. Until McMahon's visit, this confirmed atheist had prayed that after my reunion with Dad, he would confess to me and go straight. Afterward, he'd be free to live wherever he liked, perhaps even in New York, though not with my mother. Would he bring Ms. Leland?

That fantasy crushed, I called my former boyfriend,

Carlos. We'd twice seen each other at national law conferences since my graduation, and he had sent me articles on civil procedure, knowing these were more relevant to my work than to his. At our last meeting in San Diego several months prior to my Israel trip, Carlos had asked me about my dad. Then there was no news; now there's too much.

Carlos returned my call within minutes, greeting me as an old friend. Warmth and self-assurance now define him. "What can I do for you, darlin' Sally? I assume this call about an emergency is not to suggest we attend another conference together."

"Ha! I'm frantic, Carlos, and you're the first person I thought of who might give me some direction." Bringing him up to date, I asked, "Should I be worried about my legal position? I don't think I did anything wrong, but how will it look to the feds?"

"You're fine – so far. You know nothing that they don't already know. Be careful. If your father does contact you and you keep it from them, you could be vulnerable. Look, I have some advice you might not welcome. In your shoes, I'd cooperate with the FBI in return for their commitment to avoid unnecessary violence in capturing him."

"Oh, my God, you think they would hurt him, kill him? Daddy hasn't been tried for any crime. How can he be labeled a fugitive?"

"You're a lawyer, my friend. So you know better than that. You were told Interpol is on the lookout for him. That three countries have signed on. That he's been on the lam for three years. Sal, I have to return to court, am already overdue. Call me if anything else comes up. Or if you want me to be present when that FBI agent follows up with you. And Sally, when your dad surfaces and is returned to the states, if you – and he – want me to represent him, I'll be on board."

At Carlos' suggestion, I initiated contact with McMahon and got to see him within hours. Now that he knew I would cooperate, he was gracious. He thought my best bet was to work clandestinely through Alice Leland, as she was the only known contact my father had maintained.

"What I'd like you to do, Ms Marcus, is to call Ms Leland. Make sure she has all of your telephone numbers. Tell her something you know might move your father to contact you. Perhaps you are expecting a child, or have been diagnosed with breast cancer."

"You want to use me as bait to trap him." Of course, I had expected this, but hearing my own words nauseated me. Traitor!

"Think of this as saving his life. In confidence, I can assure you that he is likely to be killed by his former friends if we don't get to him first. Some of us are convinced that they are far better than we good guys are at tracking down someone they're after."

———

Jonah and I were finally together on the weekend. Having slept late, he found me in the kitchen looking through one of my family's photo albums, confiscated from the Sea Cliff house. Over coffee, we worked our way through the album, with my sharing tidbits from what seemed like some other family's past. Jonah couldn't get over how the dated pictures had no other commentary. Some were of me on horseback in a Long Island park, others of me holding up a tennis trophy. There were a few of our family, including our grandparents, like at Larry's graduations, mom forcing smiles. Several photos were of dad and me on his boat or dockside, dad relaxed, happy, in contrast to those earlier family photos where he looked glum. There was not one of mother and dad alone together.

It was time to call Alice Leland. Jonah and I had previously agreed that I would not use breast cancer – that was too creepy for a man who had lost his wife to cancer. Instead, artificially buoyant, I told Alice that my fiance and I had decided on a wedding date. Dad had missed so many occasions. I'd be devastated by his absence. At minimum, I expected him to call me. I gave Alice what I described as an untraceable throwaway phone number. She sounded free of suspicion, promising to do her best to persuade dad to call me, should he contact her. After hanging up, I felt like a rat, shocked at how good a liar I had become. Hey, I am my dad's daughter. "And," Jonah joked, "you are a lawyer!"

When I spewed out guilt and remorse, Jonah reassured me: "Your father has survived on his own for years. Even if Alice Leland is naïve, he certainly isn't. He'll smell a rat unless he's ready to be caught."

We tried to act as if life was normal. For two weeks, we each went to work, ate, slept, joined friends for tennis and dinners out. I always took the hated cell phone along, not sure what to hope for.

Tonight, while enjoying steaks with Brian and Alan at their favorite Outback, laughing over Alan's making a tragedy over the world champion Cubs falling apart this season, that phone rang. Without a parting word, I began moving like a running back, racing between tables, avoiding waiters laden with food trays, headed to the nearest bathroom. The damned phone was so deep in my purse, I almost didn't get to it in time. On the third ring, I picked up: "Daddy, it's me, Sally."

I heard sniffling before he said a word. "Baby, I miss you so much. I love you, and am so proud of you. You can't imagine how much I want to come to your wedding. Who's the lucky guy?"

"Oh, daddy, how can we fix this? I'm so scared for you."

"It's well beyond fixing, honey. No matter what it looks like, I hope you'll trust that I never meant harm." He lapsed into silence for so long, I feared he had hung up.

"Are you still there? Please, tell me how I might come visit you. I'll go anywhere, any time."

"That's impossible, Sally. You must know that I'm not free to make plans. But I promise to keep in touch. Call Alice from time to time, tell her how you are. When I can, I will call again. Remember, I love you. And am so happy you found someone to love, to love you."

With that, dad cut our connection. I sat on the closed toilet seat for several minutes, fearful of what I was certain would happen soon.

My reflection in the soiled bathroom mirror shocked me, revealing a chalk white face, belying the fifteen minutes I had devoted to making up before meeting our friends. And my right eye continued twitching even after I flooded it with cold water. With an unsteady hand, I reapplied makeup before leaving the bathroom, just as two chatting women entered.

Jonah was alone at the table. Rising, he put his arm around me, and wordlessly escorted me from the restaurant. Our friends, knowing I would need privacy, had left without dessert.

During the ride home, I sounded hysterical even to my own ears, as I repeated, "What have I done to my father? He'll be arrested, go to prison, die in prison. It's all my fault!" I hated myself, rejecting Jonah's attempt to reassure me. I was irritated that he even tried.

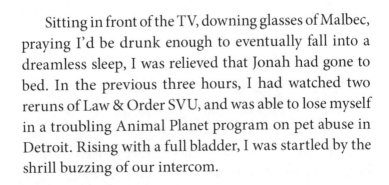

Sitting in front of the TV, downing glasses of Malbec, praying I'd be drunk enough to eventually fall into a dreamless sleep, I was relieved that Jonah had gone to bed. In the previous three hours, I had watched two reruns of Law & Order SVU, and was able to lose myself in a troubling Animal Planet program on pet abuse in Detroit. Rising with a full bladder, I was startled by the shrill buzzing of our intercom.

The following morning, Jonah described what he was confronted with when awakened by the continued attempts of our doorman to reach us. I had not answered the buzzer, instead went into the bathroom, staying there until Jonah forced me out. I emerged still wearing my jeans pants suit, eyeliner smeared and hair dripping wet.

Jonah whispered to me: "Robin McMahon is in the living room. He's waiting to speak to you, Sally. You must pull yourself together!" He then took me back into the bathroom, toweled my hair and combed it, and wiped my face clean. By this time reasonably conscious though with a dull headache, I was led by Jonah into the living room.

"Ms. Marcus, please sit down. I have news for you, good news, I believe. Your father is in custody in Bath, England. He has been hospitalized – just as a precaution because he complained of chest pain. We're hoping he'll waive extradition on discharge."

I found myself staring at this man who was remarkably alert at 2am, studying his impeccable French blue shirt and elegant silk tie, both complementing his navy pinstripe suit. Should we offer him coffee?

"Look, I know it's late. I've startled you. I also know you didn't just return from your evening out. But I need you to be attentive." He spoke sharply, then softened, perhaps regretting his tone. "You've helped us and your father with what you did. We would appreciate your help again."

"What now?" I hated him.

"I'd like you to persuade your father to cooperate with us, to waive his right to fight extradition. His challenging our request would take time, but inevitably we'd win. It'll be easier for him if he returns voluntarily."

"Dad needs to talk to an British lawyer before making that decision. We have a lawyer here who will represent him once he returns to the states. Whatever dad decides, it's his choice, not mine. Not my brother's. Not yours! But I definitely want to visit him right away."

"Agreed. Get some sleep. Here's the address and telephone number of the hospital where he's being held under police guard. I'll accompany you on a Tuesday evening flight."

I was now awake and surprisingly sober. Jonah, who must have heard the front door being chained, rejoined me. I filled him in. At my request, he placed a call to his English friend, and I called Alice Leland. After these calls, we compared notes.

Ms. Leland is furious with me. Of course she knows that I was complicit in dad's arrest – and she's guilt-ridden to have been the gullible go-between. But she did agree to find a local criminal attorney to speak to dad – hopefully today. And she will head to Bath a-sap, so he won't be alone. She knows that we are planning to visit Wednesday morning.

Jonah: "I can arrange to go with you, if you want me to…"

"No, no! I have to do this alone, or with Larry, if he can get past his hatred of dad." Realizing that I had shouted, I lowered my voice: "Jon, I appreciate your offer. You mean well but I must do this myself. Please understand." He nodded, went to bed without further conversation.

I was wide awake for the balance of the night, washing floors, doing laundry, watering plants and scheduling online payments for bills that were not yet due. At 7 am I called Larry. His first response, "Why the devil didn't you call me earlier? You know I get home from digs at 2-3 in the morning!" Of course, how dumb was I? Tears followed.

"What's going on with you little sister? Did you and Jonah call it quits?"

"Our father is in custody – in England. He needs us, Larry. I need you. Come with me, please."

"He has no god-damned right to expect anything of me. But you, that's different. Whadda you want? Money? That's about all we ever got from him." At this point, Larry sounded awake. Anger does that for him.

"Come with me. Please. Robin McMahon will accompany us Tuesday night. I'll fly into New York tomorrow – oops, that's today – and meet you at JFK at 5. Don't tell mom yet. We'll call her once we know what's happening." Relieved at his acquiescence, I was able to sleep.

On awakening in the empty condo, my thoughts traveled to meeting dad. How would he look? Would he be furious with me? Relieved that his running days were over, so able to forgive me? He'd always been an optimist, even when others were certain of disaster, like whenever Israel was threatened. Could he bring that mind-set to his crisis?

I had an urge to speak to someone - not to my brother again, what with his contempt for dad. I decided on Betty. At the stroke of 9 a m, I called her. She was gracious, surprised but grateful to hear from me about the man she loved. We spoke for more than twenty minutes, bypassing her timely attendance at a faculty conference. Before our goodbyes, I told her that I would convey her good wishes to dad. This, even though I knew that he is unlikely to give a damn, given his relationship with Alice Leland, and his current predicament.

My Stanford friend Leslie called. She wondered how I was, then invited me to Ann Arbor for a weekend. Conversation with this normal young woman left me feeling even crazier, unable to answer, "How's your family? I know your dad was ill, unable to attend graduation. Hope he's well." Relieved at the close of our conversation, I volunteered that I was headed for England with my brother. "Have a great time, Sally. And take me up on my invitation." It's a struggle to remember all my lies.

CHAPTER 16

Larry and I, both groggy after the night flight, two-hour train trip and Ambien-induced sleep, were escorted into the Bath hospital waiting room by Robin McMahon. To his credit, McMahon stayed behind while my brother and I crept down the immaculate hallway past the nurses' station toward Room 204. The small hospital was bustling with their morning activities: meal carts, physicians in and out of patients' rooms, and a few hardy men dragging IV bottles – all creating a short-lived sense of normalcy. But what was not normal was the buxom uniformed police woman sitting guard outside dad's room. She asked for our passports, following which she opened the door, admitting us.

Whispering, "Do you want to go in first, or should I?" received Larry's answering grimace and gentle shove as together we ventured into the single bedded, sunlit room. Then I saw him. Daddy was sitting in a chair, feet raised, eyes closed, a blanket on his lap. The physically powerful, heavy-set man I remembered was gone; in his place was someone much older than his years, drawn, shrunken, ashen beneath his olive complexion. Larry seemed almost tender, touching dad's shoulder, announcing: "It's Larry and Sally to see you, Dad."

Opening his eyes, grabbing Larry's hand, dad began

crying, while shaking his head: "I'm so sorry to put you both through this." He repeated this statement even as he struggled to gain control. We sat on his bed, facing him. I struggled to speak a few tender offerings before tackling dad's dire situation.

"Daddy, I know you met with Alice Leland's lawyer yesterday to discuss the question of extradition. Have you decided what you want to do? Would you prefer to fight here, or return with us as soon as you're medically cleared?" He didn't immediately respond to my question, but continued staring at me, his eyes cloudy. "You're so pretty, Sally. I'm not mad at you, honey."

I was willfully confused before acknowledging to myself that he was referring to my setting up his capture. Alice Leland must have given him the whole sordid story. Now it was my turn to tear up, to hug him, to express my love, to explain why I did what I did. Both men remained silent during my soliloquy.

More composed following a bathroom visit, his sparse white hair now combed, dad showed traces of his old self via his firmer tone: "You're forgiven. My capture was inevitable. They were always a half-step behind me. And the others, well, they too… Look, about your question, I'd better go back. Fighting here is a lost cause, a waste of time and money. Very hard on Alice. Tell the g-man who came with you."

Larry asked whether dad's health would permit travel. This got an ironic laugh from our father: "I've had bypass surgery, shunts twice, am on heart and cholesterol meds. Dying would have been a relief. I'm as strong as ever, so unfortunately can withstand a trip to New York, if that's where they're taking me."

Robin McMahon had informed us that the U.S. Attorney of the Southern District of New York would be handling the prosecution, not for treason, which is almost never prosecuted in the U.S., but for our father's selling classified information and government restricted equipment. This news posed no surprise to our savvy father, who knowing the equipment is now legally saleable to Israel, seemed convinced he could be acquitted on a technicality.

Cleared medically, dad was given his street clothes on the morning of our departure. His custom-made chocolate brown suit hung on him. And my normally fastidious father failed to notice a subtle stain on the pocket of his beige linen shirt.

Our group – dad, a deputy, Robin McMahon, Alice Leland, Larry and myself, boarded a midday British Airways flight to JFK. On joining us at the airport, Ms. Leland had ignored my brother and me, focusing her attention on daddy. Once aboard the aircraft, Larry was seated at the window, Ms. Leland in the middle, myself on the aisle. I tried to engage her. No surprise, she ignored me, pretending to concentrate on her novel, 'On Chesil Beach." I had read it years before – so stupidly mentioned that my book group had an interesting interpretation of the couple's failed sexual relationship. No response.

My own attempt to read or to sleep proved impossible. Lucky Larry, sleeping away the trip. Then again, he's used to sleeping days. Somewhere between considering Jonah's suggestions about my job problems, my memories of our family's trips many years ago to and from JFK to drop dad off or pick him up, surfaced. Mom had wanted me to accompany them. Now I understand that my parents used me as an intermediary. From dad: "What would you like me to bring you this trip, Sally?" Or from mom: "We'll get you a haircut on the way back." (This, even though I had been present when she made the appointment.) On his leaving us – he always drove – he lectured mom: "Be careful with my car!" His car, how's that? And she was a wreck driving it, usually garaging his Cadillac Escalade once home, not touching it until dad's return when typically she begged Uncle Philip to pick dad up. Why didn't she buy her own car? A smaller one more comfortable for her. They certainly could have afforded it. And why, given how angry she often was, did she not deal with him on these issues, and on her later conviction that he was not telling the truth about all those international trips?

Mom had never, to my knowledge, raised these questions with her husband. At least not that I ever heard. Perhaps for years she didn't allow herself to think dangerous thoughts – that is, until she found his passport with all those strange trips, and had that troubling experience with dad in Morocco. I can forgive the teenager I was for not demanding answers following my own two strange experiences overhearing my father, once at home in his den during that weird telephone conversation he had with Mr. Stein, and again in Israel, with dad and those Arab men secretly conversing at the King David Hotel.

Mom and I had chosen avoidance to preserve the status quo. That thought got me wondering if there was anything I do now to avoid the threat of change. At this idea, my body tensed, and I found myself biting my lips. Thinking about others is so easy. About me, scary. What don't I want to think about?

I, Sally, order you to be honest with yourself!' As my thoughts jumped from scene to scene, safely in the distant past, I ordered: 'Stop it! Stay present!'

Exhausted, after breakfast I fell into a deep sleep, just about an hour before landing. Awakened by the various announcements concerning our imminent arrival, I was briefly disoriented before forcing myself onto the bathroom line. Neither Ms. Leland, standing in front of me, nor I, acknowledged one another.

CHAPTER 17

Surprise and pleasure were competing on our mother's face as she greeted Larry and me in her condo on this dreary, damp afternoon. Larry had called her, not mentioning that I was in town, and of course, he hadn't said a word about developments with our father.

Mom's first inquiry, "What brings you to New York, Sally?" was followed by: "I hope everything's all right, honey." Though it was then past her dinner (we had stopped off at SaraBeth's after landing) – mom insisted that we partake of her delicious brisket. In the cozy kitchen, sitting close together while pretending to eat, Larry, in his typical take-charge style, began:

"Dad's in custody in New York. We just accompanied him on the flight from England. He waived extradition. He's been taken to a federal holding facility in Manhattan, where he'll remain awaiting trial. That's months off. We can see him on a prearranged schedule."

"Oh, thank God he's safe. Is he well? Depressed? Oh, how I dreamed of this, that he'd be back with us."

Sally's turn to jump in: "Mom, don't jump to conclusions. I collaborated with the FBI to trap him. He's in very serious trouble. Remember my old boyfriend, Carlos – from Stanford – well, he's a criminal defense attorney. I've asked him to see dad, to represent him, assuming dad agrees. He's flying in late tonight, and I'll take him to meet dad tomorrow."

"He's going to represent Sam? Is he qualified? I want the best – cost be damned. Maybe we should use Uncle Philip's lawyer."

"No, mom. Carlos is qualified to practice at the Federal Bar. He knows his stuff. Trust me with this, please." Mom nodded. She may have remembered that her daughter is an attorney.

How to address the trickier issue of Alice Leland? At the restaurant before coming to their mother's, Larry and Sally had discussed how to handle this - ad nauseum, with Larry getting increasingly annoyed at his sister's obsessing. Using her brother's tactics, Sally spoke:

"Mom, along with the FBI agent and us, dad was accompanied by his lady friend. She was an involuntary assist, along with me, in dad's capture. The woman truly cares for him – detests me for my part. She and dad have been a couple for several years." Shaking inside, Sally watched her mother's face for clues to her feelings.

"Your father always did have women – so that's nothing new. Don't worry, Sally. I won't fall apart. It's been years since he vanished. I have a good life without him."

Why couldn't her children believe her?

Carlos lifted Sally up with a powerful hug at their

reunion. The following day they would head to the Metropolitan Correctional Center, where she was to introduce Carlos to his future client. Her friend asked some key questions: "Has he spilled anything to the Feds or to anyone else, as far as you know?" Getting reassurance from Sally, Carlos grunted his approval: "Your father's no dope. No one keeping under the radar for years could possibly be dumb enough to rat on himself."

After being searched at the Center, passports and driver's licenses scrutinized, they were kept waiting for a half-hour before being admitted to an interviewing room. Carlos and Samuel Marcus had never met. As planned, Sally left them alone. She and Carlos were to meet up briefly at Aunt Lily's apartment, where Carlos would be staying while her aunt was vacationing in Italy.

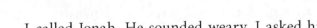

I called Jonah. He sounded weary. I asked him if anything was wrong.

"How long will you be in New York, Sally? I'm hoping you'll fly home tomorrow evening."

"Something's not right. You sound different."

"I have upsetting news. This afternoon, Angel somehow got away from Moira; she ran into traffic and was killed instantly."

"Oh, no!" I began weeping, joined by Jonah. We didn't say much; how could words help? Then Jonah began to speak: "Anne and I bought Angel just weeks before she was diagnosed. That 2 ½-pound puppy kept us sane through those horrific times; afterward, well, she was a comfort to me, a connection to Anne."

I was relieved that Jonah was sharing his pain, not forcing himself into his usual caretaker/doctor role. Ashamed, I also was jealous, hearing his still powerful connection to his late wife. It seemed that Angel's death had reactivated so much personal pain for Jonah, almost as if he was reexperiencing Anne's death. Thank goodness I succeeded in pushing aside my selfish thoughts to comfort him. We stayed on the phone for close to an hour, with my reassuring him that I would return to Chicago tomorrow night. Even after we said goodbye several times, Jonah found reasons to maintain the connection.

I was surprised when Carlos, from my aunt's, called me around midnight. He was exhausted, having been awake the previous night leaving instructions on his California cases before flying to New York.

"Sally, please trust me enough not to ask your understandable questions. I will tell you what I can, when I can. Your father opened up to me. He and I will be meeting again tomorrow before I return to San Francisco. I will follow up on what he already shared. Discovery will take weeks, even months, from their end and from ours. I'm not going to sugar coat it for you.

There's plenty to worry about. Your father's no angel. We do have to wait 'til they give us what they have – only then will we know the extent of what we're dealing with. Okay?"

"I get that I can't ask you anything – that I must trust you. I do, but it's gonna be hard."

"Another thing. I reminded your father that he was not to share with you or your brother – anyone, for that matter – anything that might incriminate him. He's smart, alert, cooperative. We need to keep him healthy and optimistic. So I do want you, the rest of the family, friends, to visit him regularly. Make certain that they know that they must stay in neutral territory. I promise to keep in close touch with you as the point person, and when possible, I will tell you what I can."

"What about my mother? They're still married, so she can't be forced to testify. Should she visit? She's very anxious to see him."

"That's up to him. From what I gathered, your father is not inclined to view her as his wife, legalities notwithstanding. I spoke to his lady friend to explain to her that she must not ask questions. She has no protection. In fact, she knows too much already, and will be called to testify. The FBI heard plenty when they tapped her phones."

"Alice Leland sees me as a pariah. But I can't help wondering why she put up with dad when she knew he was involved in illegal activities, and could get her in trouble as a collaborator."

"Don't assume your father's all bad, Sally. All we

know so far is that he conducted some business he probably shouldn't have, then eluded capture. We have to hope that his motivation was patriotic."

I couldn't help smirking. "That's how you defense attorneys can represent the worse people, even killers, and imagine they're innocent."

"Come now, don't exaggerate what I said to mean that I always impute wonderful motives to all my clients. But Sam Marcus, well, it's just possible we'll eventually see his behavior in a more kindly light."

After a brief pause, Carlos announced that he was headed for a shower and bed.

Following a late lunch on Sunday afternoon, Carlos and I taxied together to JFK. Past security, we went our separate ways, but not before Carlos reminded me that he needed a twenty thousand dollar retainer.

Jonah called me just as I was about to board my flight to Chicago. He was in the ER with a cardiac patient, thus couldn't pick me up at O'Hare.

I had anticipated being at least mildly upset at not being greeted by Angel on my entering the apartment. But what I encountered was more of a shock: nine adults were sitting in the living room, drinking wine, snacking, chatting. They had visited with Jonah until he had to leave for the emergency, then decided to remain when he told them I was headed back. His friend Allen hugged me; others followed suit. I knew most of them, with the exception of Jonah's newest colleague, Yael, and her bond trader husband, whose name I don't remember. I couldn't help noticing that Angel's regular walker was absent. She must be devastated.

On the teak console table opposite the sofa was an 8"x 10" photo of Angel. Under it, someone had put a red ribbon with the words, "We'll always remember you with love.' One of the neighbors, Doris, began speaking of pets she and husband Bruce had lost, which he insisted would never impel him to adopt another dog. She strongly disagreed. Others shared their pet stories, during which I entered my own private reverie, remembering a young, healthy Duchess.

Conversation had shifted to decorating and job searches. All that stopped on Jonah's return. Perhaps they felt guilty about the party atmosphere. At any rate, they hugged Jonah and left. He seemed okay, relieved that his elderly patient, having survived, was being monitored in ICU. He'd check on her during morning rounds.

Normally, Jonah set his alarm for 6 am, and reset it for my 7 am wake-up. On Friday, when I awakened, my bedroom clock read 8:25. Oh, my God, late for work after having been away for a week. I threw on some clothes without showering, did a rapid makeup job, and thought, 'So there's some good at not having a dog to walk.' The thought left me feeling like a traitor to Jonah, as I jogged to my bus stop.

On my arrival at the office, the receptionist announced, "Mr. Bennett wants to see you immediately!"

Judge Rand's administrative secretary was a cold fish whom few people liked. He was the one giving us our work, and I must admit he was pretty even-handed about that. But my sense was that he never liked me.

"I'm sorry to be late, Mr. Bennett. I plan to work overtime to catch up. It's been a difficult week." I had never had a private conversation with the man, who knew nothing of my family problems.

"Please sit down, Ms. Marcus." He motioned to the chair facing his desk, rather than where I had typically sat on the sofa. Uh, oh, there's gonna be a tough conversation. I'm about to be yelled at.

"It's been clear to us that you have been preoccupied with matters not relevant to our work here. I hope you'll agree that we've been remarkably patient over these months, giving you leave as needed, even limiting your caseload." He waited for my agreement, but I remained silent, so he continued: "I'm afraid Judge Rand's work has suffered to some extent, and that he cannot tolerate. He has asked me to inform you of his wish for your resignation, effective today."

Why should I have been stunned? Even having told Jonah that this might happen, I must not have believed it. Now here it was. I asked Mr. Bennett a few questions, which he answered. He had required me to complete summaries of my cases' and their current status, which I spent the rest of the day doing. Before leaving, I decided not to write a letter of resignation, considering the possibility that I'd be better off financially if they were forced to fire me. I'd ask Jonah about my options.

Will he be disgusted with me? Angry, contemptuous? But that wouldn't be Jonah's way.

I left the office around 7pm, texting Jonah that I'd be home late, without explanation. Afterward, I wandered into Trio's, an attractive neighborhood cocktail lounge, one I had noticed but never entered. The place was filled with my contemporaries on this Friday evening. Two guys offered to buy me a drink. One, an athletic Larry look-alike, succeeded in engaging me in conversation.

"Hey, what's a beautiful gal like you doing here alone on a date night?"

"I'm waiting for my husband."

"Yeah, me too. Where's your wedding ring? What's your name? Mine's Eric."

"So, Eric, you're cheating on your wife? Or at least hoping to…"

"Yeah, like you. We're both liars. But you're prettier. You work around here?"

"As of now I'm a lady of leisure. An unemployed lawyer."

Eric and I bullshitted and flirted for another half hour. I allowed him to buy me a mojito, but soon afterward insisted that I must go home. He seemed stunned when I refused to give him my phone number or to tell him where I live. He asked me what he had done to deserve such rejection, not believing the marriage lie. I had been disloyal to Jonah, especially after admitting to myself that I might have liked to spend the evening with Eric. He amused me, made me feel young, attractive, cool.

What would it be like to be free of all commitments? Jonah. My family. Financial concerns. Strolling the half-mile to the condo, my thoughts wandered between how to tell Jonah about my firing, and whether to announce my intent to stay in New York going forward. My meandering thoughts on the recent flight bringing dad to New York returned.

Perhaps Amy had been right. I had grabbed at Jonah's offer to move in with him, to live in Chicago, to take this job that I hadn't truly enjoyed. Those were scary, unwelcome thoughts. But I have begun to believe, necessary.

CHAPTER 18

For three weeks, life was eerily quiet. Jonah had not blown up at me over my being fired, but maintained a new distance. My two short visits to New York and my fears over what could happen to dad, both allowed me to ignore what I later understood was Jonah's struggle to manage his dissatisfaction with me.

An unexpected event shifted the tenuous balance. On an evening when Jonah and I attended a lecture based on Fareed Zakaria's "The Post American World,' we ran into Dr. Held. I had not seen him since I lost my job, having told him that my frequent trips to New York made therapy appointments impractical, and that without a job I could no longer afford him. Dr. Held had offered to lower his fee, and to be available if and when I called.

Leaving the auditorium, Jonah flipped out on me: "Sally, you did it again! You never told me you stopped therapy."

With that, he marched out of the building toward the crowded parking lot. For a moment, I thought he was going to drive off without me. I caught up with him as he was opening the driver's side door, then had to remind him to unlock my door.

"Jonah, Please, life has been insane. I thought I told

you. I never, ever meant to keep such a secret. Why would I?"

"Why? You have yet to consider us a couple. My colleagues are more communicative." With that, he slammed his door, said not another word to me 'til we arrived at the condo. Then, "Get out," said before he drove into the garage.

Once in the apartment, I poured us two glasses of Shiraz, demanding an explanation. I got one, but not what I expected.

"I'm not happy anymore, Sally. You're headed for New York. Stay there for now. We should take a break."

"You're having an affair, Jonah." I waited, studying him. For a half-second, he looked away, fueling my suspicion. Then, resuming eye contact, he spoke in a more measured tone.

"I haven't had an affair, though I have been tempted. You can be sure I'd never cheat as long as we're together. But even my fantasizing that, not for sex, for companionship, that's telling both of us something is seriously wrong. We need to fix us, or go our separate ways."

We sat in silence until I impulsively attempted to leave the apartment. He stopped me: "You're not going anywhere so late on this freezing night. Listen…if we've made a mess of things, maybe we can do better. We could ask Dr. Held if he'd be willing see us together."

But could I trust Jonah going forward? "My father fucked his way around the globe, now you're telling me you've been thinking of doing the same? And you want me to let down my walls?"

"Yes. There's a difference between fantasizing and cheating. I think you've often behaved with me as if you were convinced I had done the deed."

During recent visits with my father, he had not seemed depressed. Rather he showed an emotionless demeanor. Where was the volatile, aggressive guy I grew up with, the man who devised the schemes he executed, evading the police of three nations? The fighter in him must surface if he is to be a strong partner in his own defense. So stated Carlos. During our visits, I struggled to initiate conversation with dad which circumvented the subject most on all our minds.

"Dad, you're looking well. How are they treating you here?"

"No complaints. I've got enough to eat, reading material, television."

"Do you have much contact with the other men awaiting trial?"

"No, I have no interest in them. They probably feel the same. We all have plenty of trouble ahead of us." He didn't appear sad or anxious, in fact showed no observable emotion.

"You seem to be holding it together pretty well. Better than I would under the circumstances."

"You think I should fall apart? There's no reason for

that. I'm getting a nice amount of visitors, you included. Your mother was here a few times, and Larry with his family. Also, your Uncle Philip twice. He survived prison, didn't he?" I noticed that he didn't mention Alice Leland, likely his most treasured visitor. Larry told me that she had returned to London to work, would periodically come for weekend visits until the trial, when she would have to testify.

"What was it like seeing mom after so many years?"

"She looks good. Lost all that weight I was always yelling at her about. She came nicely dressed, hair colored, made up. A new woman. Maybe my leaving did her a world of good!" Dad brightened, enjoying his own humor.

"Yes, she recovered, but only after months of being depressed. That's all in the past. Did she say anything about Aunt Lily and Uncle Bob?"

"No, nothing." I was struck by his failure to follow up on my question, but then was relieved, feeling stupid to have mentioned it.

"Dad, whatever happens here, you'll handle it. You were always such a strong guy."

For all my verbal support, internally I was sad and irritated with my father's lack of interest in my life. Was he aware that my being in New York on weekdays suggested that I wasn't working? His lack of curiosity about me fueled my next statement.

"I've been fired. You remember I told you that I was working for an Illinois Supreme Court Justice in Chicago? I had been planning to leave at the end of a year – but they beat me to it. So I'm at leisure, being supported by mom for the first time since law school."

"You'll be fine." With that, dad began busying himself with a book he was reading, Larson's 'Devil in the White City." He'd had enough of me.

"You seem ready to settle down with that book, daddy. I read it years ago – it's excellent – enjoy. So I'll say goodbye for now. Okay?" I was hoping he'd say, no, stay, but nothing of that sort happened. Instead, he nodded, gave me a light kiss on the cheek as we said our goodbyes.

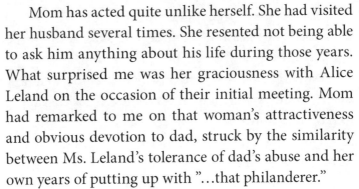

Mom has acted quite unlike herself. She had visited her husband several times. She resented not being able to ask him anything about his life during those years. What surprised me was her graciousness with Alice Leland on the occasion of their initial meeting. Mom had remarked to me on that woman's attractiveness and obvious devotion to dad, struck by the similarity between Ms. Leland's tolerance of dad's abuse and her own years of putting up with "…that philanderer."

"Sally, I used to ask myself why I went along with what he did, how he spoke to me. Now I get it. Your father was always such a dynamic guy when he chose to be social, where I thought myself dull and unattractive. Maybe we both believed that his financial success gave him a wide berth to do whatever he chose. But I was constantly furious. Now I see that I never demanded that he shape up. I was afraid he'd leave me. And I never thought beyond the women; the other stuff, that would never have occurred to me."

"Of course no one suspected him of such crimes, mom. When I dared to wonder what he was up to years ago, you didn't want to hear it. It's just not something most ordinary people have any experience with. How were we supposed to imagine him involved in treasonous activities?"

"I hate that word! Your Aunt Lily said something to me years ago – about Sam's passport. That he had to have some not-good reason for going to those dangerous places. She was sure it wasn't for romance. Afterward, I regretted having told her about the passport."

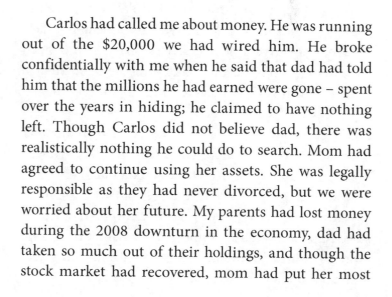

Carlos had called me about money. He was running out of the $20,000 we had wired him. He broke confidentially with me when he said that dad had told him that the millions he had earned were gone – spent over the years in hiding; he claimed to have nothing left. Though Carlos did not believe dad, there was realistically nothing he could do to search. Mom had agreed to continue using her assets. She was legally responsible as they had never divorced, but we were worried about her future. My parents had lost money during the 2008 downturn in the economy, dad had taken so much out of their holdings, and though the stock market had recovered, mom had put her most assets into bonds, so she was not benefitting that much from the tremendous market upturn. We had all urged her to have a new advisor – but she stuck with dad's friend at Merrill Lynch.

Larry and I initially agreed to pitch in, each committing our $15,000 annual inheritance from our grandparents; however, with my unemployment, I had to rescind my offer.

Carlos called to alert us to the Criminal Investigating Unit of the U.S. Internal Revenue Service beginning a search for dad's money. The IRS could do the expensive asset search our family couldn't finance. Located funds would be seized. Grim prospects for the Marcus clan.

Meanwhile, my private life was on hold. When not with my niece and nephew, now in school full-time, thus unavailable except on weekends, or with Aunt Lily who was teaching full-time, I couldn't bring myself to contact friends in New York. Was it shame about dad? Personal embarrassment that I hadn't kept in touch with these people? Or more likely, my being miserable over everything. That includes dad, Jonah and me, no job or prospects of one, depending on mom to support me. So no source of pride. It was hard to remember ever feeling so low, and for good reason. I had screwed everything up. That can't be blamed on dad. I'm trying a new strategy - to avoid looking outside myself to explain my fate. With nothing much to distract me, I stayed up late watching mindless television, then slept away mornings, 'til mom, disgusted with me, knocked, with a loud "Get up already!"

CHAPTER 19

Jon's response my planned visit, "Okay, so you're coming," didn't even sound like the guy I once knew. So when he asked me to accompany him to his favorite antique shop to pick out bedroom lamps, I agreed. Damn, my cell phone rang on our entering Curio-Alley.

"Sally, this is Jamie – Jamie Fisher. Well, not Fisher anymore, of course. I'm so relieved to have reached you."

"I've thought of you often, Jamie, and should have called months ago. Please forgive me. But this isn't the most opportune time for a chat. I'm shopping with my boyfriend. Can I call you back?"

"Please – just a few minutes. There's trouble. You know about it. Dad called to say you visited him; he gave me your number. He's a wreck."

"I should have called your dad to fill him in. He was very gracious to Jonah and me when we were in Israel. Please tell him that my father is in custody in New York. We're relieved – now at least we can help him."

"Gee, Sally… Dad and I always admired your father. He's so smart, such a take-charge guy. I used to wish my father was more like him. Daddy said many times, 'Sam Marcus is a powerhouse. Nothing gets by him.' But you must be wondering why I'm calling now. It's 'cause daddy will be testifying at your father's trial. Did you know that?"

"Oh, my God, Jamie. I should have guessed – but… well, I didn't know. Now it's my turn to ask you if you were aware our fathers were in business together. So maybe your father is cooperating with the FBI to avoid his own indictment. Of course, they could go after him anyway."

Silence followed my comment. Then she spoke softly, hesitating: "Sal, I don't know much. I haven't asked daddy anything. Years ago, when I did ask, he never gave me a straight answer. In fact, once he said I was better off not knowing – and I remember his exact words: 'Thank God your mother's gone; this would have killed her.' Daddy is full of guilt. Knowing him, I find it hard to imagine how he'll get past whatever it is."

After another prolonged silence, Jamie and I agreed to stay in touch. She volunteered her married name and address in Louisville, Kentucky. "O"Hara. Daddy loves Roy, but still hasn't quite gotten over my marrying an Irishman. And living so far away, expecting our first child, that's a killer. But he's the one who moved to Israel."

Jonah, obviously irritated with me, precipitously ended our shopping expedition, leaving to play poker with his guy friends. As is unusual these days.

Sitting over coffee in a nearby diner, my thoughts shifted between our family disaster, including my personal vulnerability to public shame, and to Jonah's hostility. Can we turn things around? I'm not so sure. Do I want to try? Freedom attracts, but also scares me.

———————

Miri is in New York. She flew in from Israel without having alerted me beforehand. She had already visited our father. Her mother was disturbed by Miri's decision to leave her job, with little money and no plan for where she'd stay in New York. Miri countered my concern: "Israelis are used to dropping in on friends of friends, to not planning everything in advance. My mom must have caught the American obsession with practicality when she lived here for grad school."

"Miri, you're a real nut! I don't live in New York, so can't house you. You haven't met my mother; for sure she'll have feelings about you – not toward you, but about her husband's fathering a child he never thought to tell her about. So we can't ask her to put you up."

I tried to come up with a plan while Miri chattered on about her visit with dad. I interrupted this recital: "My Aunt Lily always comes through for me. She might even enjoy having you – but has been putting Carlos up in her place –that's dad's lawyer – when he comes to town. I'll call her about you."

Batya had wired her daughter a little money after Miri reported having overnighted in a fleabag hotel near the Bowery without asking anyone about the area beforehand. Even Miri now acknowledged being nervous during her one night there. I kidded her: "How do a few drunks and working girls get to scare a former Sergeant in the Israeli army?" Miri was defensive. On the other hand, she was relieved when Aunt Lily came across with an invitation. East 57th Street amazed Miri, what with its crazy traffic, accompanying noise, and interesting galleries. She and Aunt Lily bonded over hot rum and cherry pie. Yuck!

I planned to return to New York the following morning. So naturally Jonah was irritated again. "Look, you can't be flying back and forth like this. You don't have a job, so must be going through whatever money you have. Why not wait 'til the trial begins? At that point being there makes sense." He cannot make up his mind – does he want me with him - or does he prefer me to remain in New York?

"I have to go. I want to see Miri. And my parents, Larry, Elisa, all appreciate my support. I need them too. You work such long hours, leaving me with nothing to do here but to obsess about everything. Including about us. Please understand!"

Jonah shook his head, hands on his hips, raising his voice: "Where do I fit in to your plans, anyway?" He didn't wait for my response, instead walked out of our bedroom, into his small home office. When I followed to protest, he shut the door in my face. How dare he treat me like this when I have such problems? A nervous wreck, I began to itch all over, scratching my arms, rubbing my eyes, nauseated.

Returning to our bedroom after a stint on the toilet, I lay on the chaise, drained, sad, confused. My rumbling stomach alerted me to my not having eaten much today. So I dragged myself to the kitchen to grab a pint of coffee ice cream and some cookies.

Jonah entered my space, standing over me like a frustrated parent, asserting self-control, his words a counterpoint to his earlier message: "Maybe I have become self-centered, Sally, but I think not altogether wrong in asking you to consider how you're dealing with this situation. Let's make a deal: you decide how often you must be in New York, and I'll agree not to blow up at you again – if you honor the deal. We must have a more predictable life if we are to stay together. Agreed?"

"It sounds okay, but..."

"I don't want 'buts'. It's not fair to me. I feel too neglected, too angry."

We left it there. I suggested we go for dinner at a new Greek restaurant, my treat. Jonah drove. After parking, he marched ahead of me and was already following the hostess to a table when I entered.

"If you're gonna be nasty, Jonah, what's the point of our being out together?" He didn't answer. When the waiter brought our menus and asked about drinks, Jonah ordered a vodka martini. He finally looked up at me: "I don't like Greek food."

"So why are we here? Let's leave." Instead, he ordered souvlaki with a lamb skewer. I followed suit. After quickly downing his martini before dinner arrived, he motioned to the waiter. "What red wines do you have?" He then ordered a bottle of cabernet. I was shocked. Jonah rarely drinks, maybe a beer with pizza, or a glass of wine when others are drinking. Nauseated, I didn't touch my wine.

We ate our dinners in silence, my stomach in knots, me wishing I possessed the guts to walk out.

Jonah never inquired about any interest I might have had in dessert. He paid the check, then walked ahead of me to the car.

"I'd like to drive, Jonah. You've had a lot to drink."

"Get in – or take a cab, if you prefer."

I remained in front of the restaurant, unsure about what next. He shouldn't drive, but was adamant about my not driving. By now he was sitting in the driver's seat, an apt metaphor for our relationship. I re-entered the restaurant to call an UBER, considering where I could go in Chicago, but knowing I would return to the apartment. Jonah was holed up in his office, door shut. I spent most of the night in the kitchen reading Rachel Kushner's "Flamethrowers." Apt, since chaos is so familiar. Against my will, I soon fell asleep on the couch. Tomorrow I escape to New York.

Carlos' email added to our troubles: "the IRS grabbed your father's money. My contacts alerted me, gracias Dios. Guess what? Your lying padre stashed three million plus euros offshore and in Switzerland. We're broke. What's your plan B?

"Why the devil did you tell Miri and her mother that I'm in prison? It's my business to decide who to tell, when to tell – not yours, young lady!" With that, dad moved as far as possible from me, pretending to read a trove of documents.

So my father joined Jonah in expressing irritation over my decisions. As in the old days, dad psychologically abandoned the object of his anger. Now it was me. Miri was to meet us here soon, forcing my hand.

"Dad, look at me, please!" He took his good time before releasing those damned papers. I motioned him to give me paper and pen, then wrote: "The IRS has all your hidden treasure." Dad paled under his swarthy complexion, shook his head as if in denial (of what?) – and wrote, "I have nothing left to fight with."

"Goddamn it – you have us to fight for. We're still your children. We love you, even if we hate what you have done to create this mess."

With rare emotion, dad offered: "I'm so sorry." Pale, sweating, saying he felt unwell, not up to seeing Miri again, to socializing. Could I intercept her, take her shopping, to a show. "Come back tonight – or better yet, tomorrow."

Miri's reaction to having her visit cancelled was not unexpected, but like a wallop: "Damn you, Sally. Who gave you the right to manage my time with daddy?" I reciprocated: "I'm sick and tired of everyone criticizing me: Jon; Dad; Carlos; you. Carlos thought I should have forced dad to tell me where the money was before the IRS tracked it; Jonah is about to dump me; daddy thinks I'm here too much and is angry that I told you his story. And now you think I should have talked him into letting you come today. Guess what? You can all take a walk." I came close to telling her to go fuck herself – but boy was I happy at my self-control when Miri hugged and kissed me.

"I'm sorry, sis. I know you've tried your hardest. This sucks. But whatever happens, we're ahead 'cause we found each other."

I asked Elisa and Larry to come into town to meet Miri. He had initially refused, but Elisa prevailed. We met at the Metropolitan Museum of Art's dining room, almost empty at this odd hour. Initially nodding to Miri, my brother left to us buy snacks and wine – and took his good time doing that. Miri and Elisa soon ran into a wall, this when Miri failed to hide her shock and disapproval – non-verbally - after learning that Elisa is not Jewish. Larry returned with goodies, acknowledging Miri. He didn't have a clue about what had happened in his absence. The mood shifted to neutral helped by the wine, and by Elisa, who never could retaliate after an attack. She reached out to Miri via questions about Israel, her family and her plans for her New York stay. And, as usual, when husband Larry remained standing – as if to take off if needed, Elisa told him, "OK, Larry dear, you need to sit down now." Larry responded, "Yeah, I know," and engaged Miri at last.

"You can imagine my reaction when my baby sister here informed me about you. Another surprise from dear old dad. One thing about Samuel Marcus – he was never boring and predictable like the rest of us." For all the joking tone, Larry's facial expression showed an emerging sadness.

Elisa and I observed the two from our own strained and separate spaces, as if at a performance in which our fate was to be decided.

Miri responded: "Sure, I understand. I don't expect you to take me as a sister so fast. But someday maybe, yes?"

Larry and Miri both had succeeded in overcoming their instinctive aggressive natures. Elisa and I relaxed. Show over. The characters – our family – had survived.

What had not been said was that each of us is vulnerable to media scrutiny. Dad, of course, for his crimes; Larry, a well-known figure; Miri, the "illegitimate" daughter; and me, the daughter who fingered her fugitive father. What drama! What spectacle! Elisa worries for her young children, who will be watching and listening to shocking news about a grandfather they do not know. How to protect them?

Miri, amused, then amazed us in minimizing her own status: "Here I am, an Israeli from Ashkelon, living here and there, with a different last name, so who will give a damn about me?"

Because museum visitors began pouring into the restaurant, it was time to leave. We taxied to Aunt Lily's, where talking freely about dad's 'activities' was safer. My brother began what felt like an interrogation: What did I know from all those visits with dad, and from my several meetings with FBI agent McMahon after our return here?

"Daddy met a few potential players casually after 9/11. Until then, his business took him primarily to customers in the state or to Canada and Mexico. Of course, he did travel with mom, and with us for our Bar and Bat Mitzvahs. I later learned, he met with you, Miri, and with your mother, in israel, on the 1997 trip for Larry's Bar Mitzvah.

"Because dad speaks fluent Hebrew, his company sent him to Israel to sell machine tools. For some reason, in spite of the company's having an international division, they also sent dad to Kuwait. That country's economy was booming following their various wars and internal political dramas, and had hard cash from petroleum exports to buy what they needed from the firm. Dad made some new contacts in Kuwait and on a side trip to Bahrain. You know that the US Fifth Fleet has an operating base in Manama there. When the Navy began major renovations from 2003 on, dad used his connections to sell equipment. All this was entirely legal, above board, within his company's extensive US government contractual agreements. So more of daddy's legitimate, authorized international business trips were to the Middle East.

"When I asked J.J. Richfield's VP why dad was given international assignments outside of Israel, he said, and I quote him: 'Sam Marcus was gifted in making crucial contacts for the company.'"

Larry smirked with his next query: "When – and how – did things go from legitimate to crooked? You're spending too damned much time on 'before' when we're all interested in 'after'."

"According to Carlos, Interpol documented that dad, beginning in 2005 – dealt with wealthy, well-connected Arab businessmen, but these men didn't themselves become 'persons of interest.' One of their sons, and in one instance, a nephew, already involved in criminal enterprise, got dad involved, a little at a time. McMahon was sure money was the draw, possibly because – and this mom never knew – dad had made large pledges to Federation and other charities that he was having trouble meeting – and, you, Larry, were at Oberlin, another big expense."

"Hey, don't blame me! Our wonderful father should have put our college money aside years before. He earned enough – but lived like a billionaire. Those pledges were to show off."

"Larry, we both know his flaws. Whatever motivated him to turn bad – will we ever truly know?"

Miri spoke up for the first time: "And he was sending money for me. Did you know that?"

"Yeah, we do now. But for Christ's sake, let's not feel sorry for the guy. A crook can always come up with why he had to commit the crime."

"Larry, back off - do you want me to continue?"

Miri appeared dejected, biting her cuticles, twirling her long ponytail. I tried, without success, to comfort this young woman who, at the moment, had a child's demeanor. Both Elisa and Aunt Lily remained silent, likely stunned by my summary. I continued:

"Dad's first potential exposure came after a French investigative journalist on a trip to the Middle East got wind of something and contacted dad's former boss. But for as much as two years, there's a gap in any information. We now know that in '06 dad began a relationship with Matti Stein, at first around legal shipments to Israel; years later, with unknown assistance from someone at his company, items not on the US government export list were sent sub rosa.

"Then, in late 2008, prior to my first year at Barnard, dad talked his old acquaintance, my friend's father, Ben Fisher, into joining his activities. Mr. Fisher had gotten himself into debt because of his wife's cancer and his daughter's tuition. Both Stein and Fisher have talked to Israel authorities and to the FBI, and both will testify at dad's trial."

An extended silence followed the end of my recital. I was drained and so were the others. Miri, squirming in her seat, I imagined was even more disturbed at hearing about her beloved uncle's involvement.

I asked the group, excluding Miri, "Where's the money to pay Carlos gonna come from? I'm tapped out. Jonah's out of the picture, including for my travel expenses. Mom is willing, but has already had to sell securities she shouldn't have in an up market."

"I guess that leaves us, sis." Turning to Elisa, Larry continued: "What's our current status? How much can we come up with, without touching the kids' college fund? I wouldn't tap into our retirement money – that would come with a stiff penalty. Savings – how much is there?"

Elisa nodded. She might not share details, but did confirm that she would transfer $50,000 to Carlos' account. I was stunned. It was my first inkling of just how successful my brother had become.

———————

Dad's physical demeanor during our visit yesterday showed his increasing strain. We had been alone in the usual visitors' space, though the always present cameras and microphones, as well as the nearby officers, make intimacy impossible.

Mom had days before brought dad photograph albums at his request. We looked at these together, beginning with brown-tinged, faded Polaroids from their honeymoon, then of baby and toddler Larry with his proud parents. After my birth there were fewer family photos, unless one counts those at events, like graduations, Larry's recitals, or my tennis award ceremonies. There was one major exception – that eventful boat trip down the intercoastal just prior to Larry leaving for Oberlin.

How excited I had been at the prospect of that trip on our modest cabin cruiser, the Lady Rhoda II. Because our parents had wanted to travel as a family before Larry was to leave home, I had been allowed to end my camp stay early. Yesterday Dad recalled that he and Larry had gotten along very well on that trip, his son willing to learn how to navigate, dad happy to give the then almost eighteen year-old responsibility.

I remember with pleasure the wonderful ports we visited: Cape May, Anapolis, the Outer Banks – and how much fun I had sleeping on our boat's narrow cots that must have felt like wombs. We ate sumptuous seafood dinners on land, fished – nauseating mom – and swam off the boat in warm, peaceful waters. That was all before our bone-chilling adventure while heading south to visit mom's parents in Boca Raton.

Larry had spotted a large, elegant cabin cruiser with six visible occupants, several of whom were waving and shouting to catch our attention. Their yacht had lost power, and was drifting out of the intercoastal toward the more intense current of the open ocean. Dad took charge, to Larry's obvious relief, steering our smaller craft at low speed as close to the other boat as was safe. Mother, for a change, was a silent observer. The tide kept pushing our boat either too close or too far from the crippled yacht, until dad was able to throw a line to the captain, who secured it. While we all watched, Larry had called in an SOS to the Coast Guard. The woman and her two young children, all wearing life jackets, boarded our boat. Mom took charge, settling the children with snacks, and taking the nervous Ginny into our galley. Whatever mom did calmed the woman. The other Captain, Milton, his teenage son and the boy's friend, all remained on their boat.

Dad had explained, during our conversation yesterday, that he had to pull the larger yacht into calmer waters closer to shore, at a very low speed. "We were within an hours' sail of Savannah, our next planned destination. After the Coast Guard arrived, they took command. "Their officer gave me credit for 'outstanding seamanship' – and sent me a plaque months later."

Once on shore, boats safe at anchor, our families had dinner together at a beautiful waterfront restaurant. The two dads and their sons bonded. I believe they stayed in touch for many years. As a child at that time, I listened to the grown-ups talk, very proud of my capable, smart father.

"You were so brave, Daddy. I remember how scared mom was that we'd crash. Were you worried?"

"Never thought like that. I knew my boat. Milton did his part. We focused on what we had to do. No time to commiserate on what might happen." After a brief silence, dad continued: "It was the first time in years that Larry and I were buddies. I don't know how things had gotten so bad between us. I guess your mom told him stuff he shouldn't have known, or he could have overheard our fights. Once he left for Ohio, whatever good that trip accomplished, it didn't last." Dad and I shared a moment of deeply felt sadness. I reached for him. He shook his head, as if to shake off the bad feeling.

"Did you ever reach out to Larry after that trip? How about now? He's visited you here. And he's so much more at peace with himself."

"He comes all right. But considering the circumstances..." Looking at the camera, he went on: "I guess he has a right to condemn me. He doesn't say much, leaves the talking to Elisa. He never comes alone, hides behind her and his kids. They're great kids. The boy – Matthew – reminds me of Larry. Doesn't say anything unless I ask him a question. Now Isabel, she's a beauty, and smart. She reminds me of you, seems to like me." Dad smiled sheepishly, shrugging as if he couldn't quite believe that.

We spoke more about past pleasant memories until dad mentioned that Boston trip. I noticed he didn't refer to his former mistress, and I didn't want to confront him more than was necessary.

"Yes, Dad, mom made a terrible mistake in taking me on that trip. It certainly didn't help me to deal with it, that neither you, nor mom, ever asked me how I was. How was it – right after Boston or even years later – neither of you thought about the possible impact of such a frightening experience on me?"

"Hey, if I had a chance to do over lots of things in my life…" Looking down, pretending new interest in his shoes, dad shook his head. "I'm exhausted, Sally. Maybe we can call it a visit." With that, he grabbed me close to him, hiding his face from my view, and began weeping.

Alone on the trip to my mother's, I asked myself why I hadn't been able to be more generous to my father. He is, after all, in such a precarious, traumatic situation. Perhaps Larry and I had both been too hurt as children to learn forgiveness. As adults, we might understand, even be much less angry, since we are no longer vulnerable. But we won't give up our right to acknowledge the old hurts. How had Larry gotten over his distrust to let Elisa in? To make close guy friends? Ask him!

I headed for Barnes & Noble, perusing some of my favorite authors' new paperbacks. But I left without buying. Reading anything longer or more serious than a fashion magazine has become impossible.

Returning to mom's apartment, I was relieved to discover she wasn't home. As is her way, she had left a note: 'Playing canasta - see you later.'

Entering the guest bedroom, I found a large, lined yellow pad from mom's desk, planning to write about my parents' relationship and about my extended family during my childhood. But those words never came. I almost gave up, until the thoughts pouring out of my pen had to do with me alone. My fears. My insecurities. My lost opportunities. Lost friendships. Loss, loss, loss. Confusion about where from here do I go to find myself. I wrote in Caps: YOU ARE YOUNG ENOUGH TO GET THERE! But where? Do I even want to be a lawyer? How did I make that decision? Had I unconsciously imagined that dad would be in trouble someday, that I could represent him? If so, what a crazy idea that was. It seems that I can't even rescue myself. No, no, no. Do not think that! Damn you, do your work.

Afterward, I fell asleep, splayed across the bed. That's how mom found me when she returned, inviting me out to dinner. Thankfully, she asked me no questions.

CHAPTER 20

Miri couldn't believe that I never met the Obamas during my time in Chicago. She thinks "...he's cute and smart and talks like a movie actor." "But Israelis didn't trust him. They trust Trump." Miri expected to be invited to Chicago, not having any idea of where Jonah and I were in our relationship. She was a riot: "When I'm there, I bet I can meet President Obama." I reminded her that the President and Michelle were still living in D.C. Reality didn't faze her.

I had left messages for Jonah. He took several days to respond. After a few superficial comments – he asked me how things were in New York, what I'd been up to – he spoke his truth: "You may be right, Sally, to think we rushed into our relationship. And it was largely my doing. I was lonely. The idea of dating repelled me. And there you were – beautiful, smart, affectionate – and Jewish to boot."

"It's not all on you, Jonah. But shouldn't we have this talk in person?" I told him that Miri was anxious to visit Chicago again, sharing her fantasy about meeting our former president. That comment did succeed in ushering in a lighter interchange between us. He said, "Bring her along. She sounds like fun." So I did. I told

Jonah that Miri and I would share the guest bedroom. He never challenged me.

Miri was amazed at the condo's stunning views of Lake Michigan and decided that Jonah must be very rich. Everything delighted her, even if the Obamas were vacationing in Hawaii. She remained convinced that had they been here, they would have welcomed her visit. She ate up a storm in the several ethnic restaurants we managed to hit during our long weekend. I paid, naturally with mom's money.

On Monday, our last full day in Chicago, she accompanied me to a boys' vocational school located in a disadvantaged minority community. I had tutored there on occasion. The 14-16 year old boys acted real tough with me, using slang I didn't understand. Without asking me, Miri took over, determined to demonstrate how a former Sergeant in the Israeli army handles kids. She had rejected what she called my psychologizing: "That's bull. You have to shut them up, tell them they can't fuck with you; teach!" I had told her that their truancy and tough attitude are defenses to cover their shame over how much they don't know. Miri giggled. "You Americans. When are you gonna learn? Don't you think we have tough kids in Israel – young gangsters? We handle them. The difference is these kids handle you." She could be right.

Miri/Sally activities took place during daytime, with Jonah working Friday and Monday, and keeping tennis and golf dates over the weekend. He joined us for evenings out at two restaurants, allowing me to treat both nights. On Sunday, I insisted that he and I carve out some private time to talk. That required that I tell Miri. She volunteered to go shopping all afternoon, laughing: "Hungry for a good lay, huh? Go for it!" If only she knew...

Though the condo was now ours alone, Jonah shut his office door on our entry. We sat facing each other, he on his swivel office chair, me on the two-seater sofa. It was as if we were at a gathering, just having met. Neither of us seemed ready to start a conversation, but as I am the more nervous talker, I began.

"We have admitted that we haven't been getting along for months. I'm so sad about everything. I've hurt you. And you have retaliated – against your own nature. We've made a mess."

He nodded. "I haven't been very nice. And I hate that your focus on the family crisis in New York has reduced me to being someone I'm not."

"Are you saying it's all me?"

"Mostly you. No one I've ever been close to has gotten me so infuriated."

"Well, my parents..." Jonah interrupted me, sharply.

"You can't continue to blame them for your behavior, Sally. Grow up! Don't tell me that all those sessions in therapy left you where you began – not taking responsibility."

"And what about you – holding me responsible for your behavior? That's not fair. You could have been more understanding."

"I thought I was, for a long time. Before and during

Israel. Afterward, while you were feeling so guilty about trapping your father. But when was my turn? You gave nothing back."

Neither of us knew what else could be said. Silence was painful as well as frightening for me. Tears flowed down my cheeks. Jonah half raised from his chair – I thought with an impulse to comfort me. But he sat back, waiting. For what? I finally spoke:

"I guess this is our Waterloo, Jonah. I will pack up before Miri returns."

Miri and I stayed overnight. Jonah left for his office before we awakened. If Miri suspected something, she exercised amazing restraint in not asking me questions I would have been unhappy to hear. After a late breakfast, we went to the Chicago Museum of Art, then to lunch and to an art film. Before our flight to New York, I texted Jonah: "Thanks for everything, including welcoming Miri."

Carlos texted me as Miri and I were in a taxi headed to Manhattan. He wrote: "Please read my email. It's an exact copy of what I wrote to you weeks after we ended our relationship - but never sent."

Intrigued but not wanting to share this with Miri, I had the driver drop her off at Aunt Lily's before I entered an uncrowded Panera's near mom's. To protect my mother from needless worrying, I texted her: 'stopped off for a while – see you in an hour.'

"SOMEDAY when we're both grounded, we'll be back together, Sal. You know that; I know that. Before everything went haywire, we were a great team, though how to overcome our backgrounds will remain a challenge when we do reconcile. That will happen, just when, we can't predict.

I LOVE your laugh, your energy, your smarts, how you are always ready for anything. And you're one sexy broad! Or at least you were all of that til we both went off the rails, you about your father's disappearance (fuck him if he engineered it) and my money problems, compounded by guilt over my family's struggles.

"DO NOT GIVE UP ON US!

You asked me a crazy question when we last were together. Why did I pick you? I had so many beautiful ladies on campus willing, ready to be with me. Because we were in such a bad place, and I thought you were nuts to put yourself down like that, I just shook my head. I refused to answer. Now I will: You are inherently lovable, genuine – besides the obvious noted above. How come you don't know that about yourself?

Stunned, I stayed put. How to compose a response? Carlos undoubtedly expected one. Why had he chosen to send this to me now? Why not years ago, when it would have meant the world to me to know he cared? True to myself, I postponed a response.

Mom was not alone, waiting for me with a superb seafood dinner, and with Aunt Lily and mom's neighbor, Beth. They were drinking Chablis when I arrived, and were delighting in a salacious story – allowing me my silence. It wasn't until Beth left to meet her hubby at the theatre and mom began her cleaning up in the kitchen, that my savvy aunt admitted she knew "…something's up. Wanna talk?"

"Jonah and I are history. I can't be in two places at once. He can't tolerate my priorities. And it's maybe true that we both jumped into the relationship prematurely, for the wrong reasons."

"Are you sure it's over? This is a helluva time to make big decisions."

"Yeah – that could be true. But somehow – though he basically made the decision – I believe it's the right one. I was too much the coward to make it for us. Sure, I was hurt that he wanted out. You know that I can't tolerate rejection. But I am relieved."

I finally emailed a response to Carlos: Why send this now? Why not then? I lay in bed in my clothes, intending to change. I was awakened by the aroma of fresh coffee; the bedroom clock read 9:10 am.

Alice Leland had resolved our financial crisis by sending Carlos "…a very big check." Dad had given her $150,000 years ago to modernize her shop. Now I wondered where she would have gotten that kind of money. Not really my business. We were all relieved by her generosity.

On my next visit to dad, he greeted me with, "How are you doing, baby? You look like hell. Don't tell me my chic daughter is following in her dowdy mother's footsteps?"

"Nice for you to put it that way, daddy. I just got over a cold."

Something I said or did, or maybe how I looked, captured his attention. His next words startled me: "You seem unhappy, kid. Is anything wrong with you and your guy?"

Dad had not asked me one personal question during any of my previous visits. His sudden fatherly interest wasn't all that welcome. Then he hugged me. That did it. I collapsed, told all.

"Just because I was a dog in heat, not every guy is like that. You gotta wait 'til he fucks up before you crucify him."

I did not appreciate dad's support of Jonah. But I asked, "Is that what I'm doing?"

"Yeah, it sounds that way to me. At least your mother had plenty of reason to treat me like shit. What's your excuse?"

So if I imagined that telling my story would get me loving support from my dad, that didn't happen. Men stick together; so do we women.

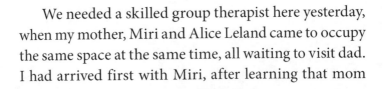

We needed a skilled group therapist here yesterday, when my mother, Miri and Alice Leland came to occupy the same space at the same time, all waiting to visit dad. I had arrived first with Miri, after learning that mom had a dental appointment. Mom and Miri had met once, briefly; it had proved an uncomfortable, frigid occasion, via mom. When Miri and I eyeballed my mother at her arrival, I worried that things could get unpleasant. But that never materialized. Instead, Alice Leland entered, shifting mom's vitriol.

"What are you doing here, Ms. Leland? Don't you have a shop to attend to in London?"

"Yes, Mrs. Marcus, I do. My daughter-in-law, knowing how distressed I am being so far away from Sam, is covering for me this weekend."

"You are not welcome here. Sam's family is his support system. I am his wife – just in case you forgot. You've met my daughter, Sally. My son, Larry and his wife will be here tomorrow with their children. My grandchildren, Sam's grandchildren."

Ms. Leland paled, silent. I wondered if she would lose her composure. The danger of that receded as this composed, attractive, slender, meticulously groomed and outfitted woman strolled to the far corner of the room. She picked up an old Newsweek, pretending to read.

It was my mother's turn to be miserable. She had put on quite a show. I knew it, as did Miri. In spite of her awful behavior, as her daughter I had to support her. But when I walked over to her, she turned away from me. She preferred remaining angry, as in the old days, combatting hurt with rage.

Four of us waited in tense silence until we were due to be checked in – two at a time. I prayed it would go well, but could not have guessed at what did happen. The uniformed black woman sitting behind a bulletproof security window requested our licenses, then left to check these against her database. On her return, she addressed Alice Leland. "We cannot admit you." Hearing this, asking, "But why not?" Ms. Leland crumbled at the guard's answer: "I have no information on that."

Seeing my mother's smirk, I was infused with an urge to smack her. But a tenderhearted Miri put her arm around mother, able to muster more compassion than I. But then she didn't have our history.

That afternoon's meeting with dad was a struggle. Not one of us would dare say a word about the prior scene, or to tell him that Alice Leland had traveled from London only to be denied entry. Dad would eventually find out, but not through us.

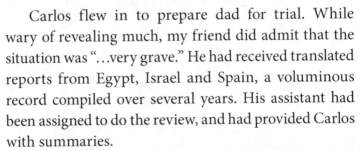

Carlos flew in to prepare dad for trial. While wary of revealing much, my friend did admit that the situation was "…very grave." He had received translated reports from Egypt, Israel and Spain, a voluminous record compiled over several years. His assistant had been assigned to do the review, and had provided Carlos with summaries.

"These reports, Sally, detail numerous meetings your father had with known international smugglers and other so-called suspicious persons. "On at least two occasions, Sam was detained for questioning, once by Egyptian police, another time by the Israelis. He was never charged. Even the Barcelona police kept an eye on him, on whose request, we do not as yet know. Why London never participated is a mystery, since that was his base. Maybe Sam was careful to avoid suspicion in England to protect Ms. Leland. At any rate, we are challenging the admission of these reports at trial, but I wouldn't count on winning that motion."

Carlos had never acknowledged potential defeat to me before today's talk. More damning would be testimony from dad's known collaborators, several of whom were telling all to mitigate their own legal vulnerability. Alice Leland would be required to testify. She may know a great deal more than others, and since the FBI had long tapped her phones, dissembling would be dangerous for her.

"Carlos, who are these other men dad was involved with? You have the reports. The list will be published – so you can tell me."

"It's possible that some of them were Mossad agents, or working with them. Sam insists that everything he did was for Israel. Two points are obvious: his activities in Israel go back a long way, and eventually became quite lucrative; and they accelerated and expanded geographically during the years 2012-15."

"My friend's father implied that money was dad's main motivation. But Matti Stein disagreed, telling me that dad was a patriot, doing what he did for Israel. So confusing. Will we hear from daddy at trial?"

"Not a chance. After the trial, whichever way it goes, he'll be free to answer your questions."

Carlos urged me to meet him at Graffiti, his absolute favorite New York tapas restaurant. I hoped – foolishly – that his invitation meant updates on dad's case, or was a follow up to his email. Both possibilities unnerved me. Speaking on the phone late the previous evening, we managed to avoid serious topics.

Carlos said that while we eat, we chat only about food. Okay, I'd cooperate. He ordered a chestnut bread starter enhanced by a Spanish light-bodied red wine. Awaiting our pork dumpling appetizer, I came close to violating his rule: "No heavy conversation til desert!" Then, grinning, he asked me if I'd ever eaten at a Mexican restaurant, Tortas Frontera, in Chicago, where famous chef Rick Bayless presides. "Buy one of his cook books. It'll make you a star!"

"What, in the midst of all this trouble, you decide to talk restaurants and cook books? Yes, Jonah and I took his friends there for their tenth anniversary. It was fabulous. I should have known you get around, that you've eaten in top Mexican and Spanish restaurants in every town you've ever visited. When were you in Chicago last?"

"Two years ago." Carlos ordered desert, at which point he finally decided to get serious. "We need squeaky clean character witnesses for trial. Here are a few names your father gave me. Look at them; add your own. If you disagree with Sam's list, let me know. It's not the most critical part of our defense, but important."

A wave of sadness enveloped me as I surveyed the names. My parents' oldest friends, like Anne and Jim, and others had known from mom of my father's indiscretions. They took her side, naturally, and I believed were unlikely to see my father as a good guy, in or out of court.

Carlos reached across the small table, grabbing my hand. Demanding my attention by his eyeball-to-eyeball approach, he at last referred to his email. "We need time together, Sally. You asked why I never sent that email after our break-up. I was struggling – about money – and imaging our differences were too important to ignore. Remember, I was raised Catholic, and in those years, took that seriously. You were, and are, a rich Jewish girl from New York. I half-believed that you saw me as someone to have a fling with, a liberal thing to do - before you'd commit to a guy from your own background. So I protected myself.

"And who knew that my career would ever go anywhere? Me, a poor mixed-race Mexican guy competing with all those well-connected Americans. That's why I never considered opting for a big firm. In my own practice I thought I'd stand a chance."

"But, Carlos…"

"Let me finish. You were still at Stanford, with two full years ahead of you. Where would I end up? I needed to be free to go where my work took me. Okay, speak!"

"Thanks for permission. No, I realize you had to get it out. You were wrong about me, but right about us not being able to be together then. The same could be true of us now, brought together by my father's insanity. And, not incidentally, Jonah and I have just broken up. I'm not about to jump into another relationship anytime soon."

"I understand on both counts. When this trial is over, I intend to talk you into giving us another chance. That means you taking the California Bar, getting work near me. I can't change my location, but you can, and I will help you find something interesting. Don't let's run away again, Sally. We're older, hopefully smarter. Next time, if we do elect to say goodbye, it'll be for solid reasons. So – ready to give us a chance?"

I nodded – almost against my will. What I did not tell Carlos was that Jonah had weeks ago booked us in New York for a long weekend to celebrate his 35th birthday, and we had then committed to a costly, non-refundable boutique hotel for two nights. In speaking to Jonah the previous evening, he and I elected to keep the date, as friends.

Jonah's 40th birthday weekend began in a stilted fashion, with neither of us knowing quite how to handle it. I drove us from LaGuardia Airport, grateful for the rare easy traffic, while Jonah spoke about Chicago and national politics. I filled him in on what was happening in advance of dad's trial. But it was only after we rented bikes out east, riding from Hampton Bays to Montauk, that we both relaxed.

Naturally, once in the beachfront hotel, our sleeping arrangement became an issue. We handled it – each sleeping in a Queen-size bed. The following morning saw us getting a late start, a delightfully high calorie sausage and pancake breakfast fueling our hiking the beach at Quoque. As in our more loving days, Jonah insisted on smearing sunblock all over me each time we exited the water.

We hugged a bitter-sweet goodbye following a lobster dinner on Long Island Sound, before I dropped Jonah off for his return flight to Chicago.

On the drive back into Manhattan, I answered a call from Elisa. She patiently listened to my chatter about the weekend. Hanging up, I chastised myself; each time we spoke on the phone or in person, I dominated the conversation with my stuff, not even pretending interest in what was going on with her. But I was pleased at my admitting to her that I had become the most narcissistic human on the globe. She laughed. "You're not in Trump's league yet, Sally, but you may be on your way!" Oops!

Mom waited up for me. She always worried about my driving, not because I'm a bad driver – she is fearful of whoever drives, especially her. To her credit, she did not interrogate me about Jonah. I was grateful, it being close to midnight, after what had been, for me, a physically and emotionally challenging weekend. I did

189

tell her that Jonah and I have agreed on a good ending. "I'm fine, Mom. Truly."

We stayed up 'til 3 in the morning watching reruns of Carol Burnett's show, then, Casablanca. It felt so good to laugh at her Carol's antics, but the painful separation between Bogart and Bergman was too close to my real life.

CHAPTER 21

During the weeks leading up to the trial, friends living all over the U.S. contacted me. What with online, print and television media, there had been and would continue to be impressive coverage of the shocking news about dad. My family's Sea Cliff neighbors who had admired him conveyed belief in his innocence. I didn't disabuse them of that fantasy.

Uncle Philip knew the truth, as did dad's much older sister, who had contempt for both her wayward brothers. I didn't pick up the phone without first ascertaining the call was from a friendly soul, and rarely responded to old friends on Facebook, unless about Trump @ Co.

Two days before jury selection was to begin, I retrieved an ominous phone message. In accented but decent English, a man recorded one sentence: "Remind your father that we can be more dangerous than any American prison." With racing pulse and labored breathing I telephoned Robin McMahon, then alerted Carlos. If I needed McMahon to assure me that someone was playing a macabre joke, I got the opposite: "We need to meet soon, Sally. But first I want to do a little sleuthing on my own. You know we've tapped your mother's incoming calls, so we'll have the number your caller used, though it'll be a throw-away. Please, you must be alert when you're out and about, and be sure to give your whole family a heads up on this."

"I wouldn't want to alarm my mother." He vehemently disagreed: "Hiding information from her could put her at risk."

To our family's dismay, each of the initial three trial dates resulted in postponement. That didn't help dad any, though he had been prepared for this likelihood. Finally, Carlos and the U.S. Attorney's office were set to conduct voir dire to impanel a jury. Though I had never tried a case – except for moot court during my law school days – and was sure I never would, I would have loved to watch these skilled attorneys in action. My having to testify precluded my attending beforehand.

The New York, Long Island and Jewish newspapers had caught up with the story of a local businessman in federal court on serious charges. The N.Y.Times, the Daily News, the N.Y.Post – even Long Island Newsday, all posted inflammatory headlines. After all, papers are a dying breed, so if they have an opportunity to increase circulation, they jump on it. Alice Leland had informed Carlos via email that news of dad's arrest had spread through their London papers and media.

Mother was humiliated by the media's attention, which included unwelcome telephone calls inviting her to daytime television programs, magazine interviews, even potential book deals. She worried about possible negative impact on her grandchildren, who are savvy tech kids. After terminating her home phone service, for a time she received no unwelcome messages on her cell phone.

Dad could not be protected from the notoriety. Daily, he read the NY Times and the Wall St. Journal, which was a good thing, because those sophisticated venues had fleeing interest in him. But he had his computer, considered an aid in his defense. Like most educated defendants, he had become a quasi-attorney in the months before trial, and had on occasion, attempted to get his lawyer-daughter on board.

"Sally, what would you say if I told you that it's possible that Netanyahu or someone else high up in Likud might be of help to me?"

Dad said this loud and clear, notwithstanding the microphones.

"You need to discuss your case only with your legal team. Not with me. Supervise Carlos! I know nothing, and that's the way it has to be! I wrote: Do you want the prosecutors to hear you confessed to me?" motioning in the direction of the cameras. Dad wrote: "Why would you have to talk? You're too pure for my taste." He went on to write: "Trump is in much more legal trouble than I am!" Yeah, agreed, so what?

By the time I left him, I was very worried. Was he talking to others about his case? If so, to whom? Uncle Philip was my best guess, though he's smart enough to shut dad down.

Over lunch with mom at Tony Roma's, mother confirmed my worst fears. "Your father still cares for me. He said as much. He told me some things about how he lived, what he did, even about that Leland woman. When he gets released, we'll give it another try."

"Mom, you're off the wall. First of all, he shouldn't be talking to you. They're listening – you know that. And being cornered, daddy cannot be trusted with anything he says. Remember what a skilled manipulator he is. He needs your money, your support. He's hoodwinking you into imagining a reconciliation. What are you thinking?"

I was so shaken by this crazy conversation that afterward I called Aunt Lily and Larry, pleading with both of them to talk some sense into mom - and thus handed Larry still another reason to detest our father.

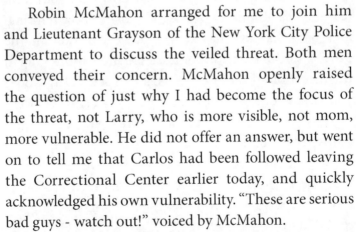

Robin McMahon arranged for me to join him and Lieutenant Grayson of the New York City Police Department to discuss the veiled threat. Both men conveyed their concern. McMahon openly raised the question of just why I had become the focus of the threat, not Larry, who is more visible, not mom, more vulnerable. He did not offer an answer, but went on to tell me that Carlos had been followed leaving the Correctional Center earlier today, and quickly acknowledged his own vulnerability. "These are serious bad guys - watch out!" voiced by McMahon.

Lieutenant Grayson, a tall, muscular blond fortyish Robert Redford look-alike, spoke carefully, addressing me: "You may well hear from them again, Ms. Marcus.

They are sending a warning to your father to limit what he tells his attorney about them. These men could be the same thugs who tried to kill him when he ventured into Cairo – a rare dumb move on his part."

In response to my query, Grayson admitted never having met my dad. "Your father's attorney must stress to him that his sharing anything with a family member could put that person at risk. You are aware that two men, one of them Egyptian, followed Marcus from the Cairo airport to a small hotel on the outskirts of the city, where, that night, they were observed planting an explosive device under his rental car, which he had parked in back of the hotel. One of them got away. The other, Abdel Ahmed, is in custody. Even our Egyptian colleagues with their creative interrogation techniques have thus far failed to get much from him." After a brief interruption during which he answered his cell phone, he continued: "Egyptian police interrogated your father, suspicious as to why he was targeted. Told that he had substantial cash on hand for a possible real estate investment, the police let him go."

How can I possibly grasp all this? Lapsing into a reverie, remote from these two cops, I stopped listening. McMahon grabbed my arm: "Sally Marcus. Stay with us! This is not the time to disconnect. Your safety, possibly your family's, depends on your courage."

"I'm a coward. Why me? Do you think they know that? My brother would be better at this."

"You've been selected, young lady. You're the point person here. We didn't pick you; they did, possibly because they know you were involved in your father's capture." With that, Lt. Grayson began detailing what I could expect and how I must handle myself.

"They will call again, perhaps hanging up without a message. They know we will have access to all family telephones, so do not use any of them, and tell that to the rest of your family. Do not tell your father anything. The FBI is counting on Marcus giving them useful information. He will not cooperate if he knows from you of the potential danger to the family.

McMahon chimed in to support what Grayson had articulated so clearly. "If Sam Marcus contributes useful information to us, that would look good for him at sentencing."

"What about federal sentencing guidelines? How much leeway does the judge actually have in these cases?"

"More than you think. Especially where prison time is served. You're an attorney, so you must know there's a range in sentencing. We could ask for leniency for a cooperating Sam Marcus."

"I take it you'd do the reverse, if he refused to help you."

"Count on it."

"Is my dad in danger from these killers?"

"He could be. We're posting extra guards in the courtroom, as well as assigning coverage for your family – from NYPD. You are to communicate with us if you hear or see anything suspicious."

There was more, much more, but I tuned in and out,

even to taking a short call from a friend. It wasn't difficult for me to interpret these g-men's facial expressions during that call, and sotto voce conversation: dismay at my behavior.

Before leaving, I managed to convey my gratitude for their help. And, clear by now about my role, accepting what it entailed, I promised them, and myself, that the time for my falling apart had expired.

CHAPTER 22

The twelve-member jury and two alternates, representing New York's dynamic cultural and gender diversity, was seated in a courtroom filled with journalists and spectators. My mother, Larry and Elisa were among them, having been screened for weapons and admitted early. Uncle Philip was planning on attending tomorrow. I was initially barred from attending as I will be an early prosecution witness.

This tense day had begun with a battle between mom and myself, this over breakfast, which neither of us consumed. She had confided in me her intent to embrace dad in front of the jury, aimed at letting them know that she fully supported him. When I objected, not in the nicest possible fashion, she retaliated: "What do you know about relationships anyway; you just wrecked one with that great guy who loved you. Don't dare tell me what to do!" My old mother returned.

The U.S. Attorney's office had advised Carlos that certain potential evidence was classified, and could not be presented at trial. They provided summaries to Carlos and his associate, but with many names and places redacted. He was not pleased.

Larry took copious notes for my benefit. The entire day was devoted to the lead prosecuting attorney's presentation of charges.

Larry's notes:

Dad had first encountered his known partner, Israeli Matti Stein, on a legitimate business trip to Israel; while they had kept in touch, having become friends, they did not venture into illegal activities for at least three years. What prompted the shift was another tunnel attack by Gaza. Dad arranged for the smuggling of top secret software and small U.S. government-approved machinery into Israel. He was paid via money deposited in a Swiss account in UBS, the first payment: $95,000. The prosecutor cracked, "Small change, given what followed." (I bet the money came from the Israeli government)

When you were with daddy at the King David Hotel and overheard his meeting with those two guys, guess what – prosecution knows about them. One is Egyptian, in jail, one Moroccan, on the run. Dad used these connections for years, and they supposedly facilitated his meeting others as well. Why dad used his own passport for those trips to Israel, and the vacation with mom to Spain and Morocco, where he was identified by local police in a meeting with one of these guys, is an open question. After each trips, dad's bank account grew. The closed UBS 'black' account which once had 2.1 million Euros, was put into evidence.

Benjamin Fisher had joined the team months prior to your overhearing that telephone call dad made to him. Fisher's role was to manage the increasingly complex financial arrangements, which included bribing airline personnel at small, remote, private U.S. airports to sign off on fictitious manifests. All payments were made in dollars.

In late 2014, dad was detained by the Egyptian police. They had him in their sights because he had been spotted with a known member of the Muslim Brotherhood, which, for all its prior political success, was still viewed by the Egyptian government as a dangerous terrorist organization. Morsi's election years before and his overthrow had produced a chaotic time in Egypt. Dad was depicted as having taken advantage of the chaos by using the country as one of his bases of operations. (ME: I was horrified to hear that MB, enemy of Israel, became dad's cover)

After dad's rental car was tampered with in Cairo, and he gave the police some bullshit story about real estate investments, one higher-up sharp cop placed dad on their watch list and consulted Interpol. It was then that Egypt learned that Morocco and Spain were also interested in him. (LARRY: Signing out)

Mom was a wreck at the end of that first day, asking me "How am I supposed to survive this? Can it all be true?" What, it was just hitting her? Struggling to maintain my own composure and to be more sympathetic, I just nodded, and suggested dinner out tonight with Larry and Elisa. My lovely sister-in-law, pale and shaky, always the protective mother, said, "I hope our kids never, ever have to learn any of this – even if what we're hearing is half true, their grandfather is a terrible man." Larry announced his escape tomorrow, heading to his daughter's dance recital. "I heard enough already!"

Please don't rush to judgment, I begged them, but knew, from my youthful personal snapshots of our father's sneaky behavior, that more, even worse, would inevitably emerge in the trial.

After dinner, Larry and Elisa went home. I was reluctant to spend the evening with mom, so decided on an ultimate escape, which I knew she wouldn't enjoy, an old Japanese art film, *Picture Bride*. Those two peaceful hours were my last for many days.

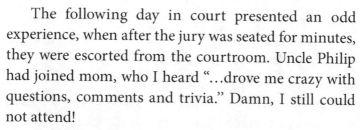

The following day in court presented an odd experience, when after the jury was seated for minutes, they were escorted from the courtroom. Uncle Philip had joined mom, who I heard "...drove me crazy with questions, comments and trivia." Damn, I still could not attend!

Finally, another prosecutor, Jay Jackson, a thirty-something, well-built, bespectacled black man whose accent suggested a Caribbean upbringing, and Carlos, began discussing something with the judge. Jackson was then joined by the lead prosecutor, Elaine Anderson, a late 40's woman attired in a stunning navy tailored Armani pants suit and white silk shirt. After they conferred, she would take charge.

The jury was escorted back into the courtroom.

I'm sure they must have been curious about what had occurred in their absence.

It was finally time for Carlos' opening argument. On this crucial day, my flamboyant friend dressed conservatively, his tall, slim figure clothed in Versace pin-striped grey, his black silk shirt softened by a wide, pale blue patterned tie. Elisa, with her special brand of shorthand, took extensive notes and typed them up for us later that afternoon.

"I want you to know my client, Sam Marcus, in a more balanced way than has been presented by the prosecution. (Carlos smiled warmly!) "After all, their task is to convince you he's the devil." (I think C had the jurors with him).

"The real Sam Marcus is a husband, a father, a grandfather, a lifelong resident of New York, who up until seven years ago led an imperfect, but not atypical life for a successful businessman. He lived with his wife in Sea Cliff, L.I., supported her and his daughter, who was at Stanford Law School. He had welcomed into their home his son and daughter-in-law and their infant daughter, on their return from the Midwest. He traveled extensively as national sales manager for his firm, J.J. Richfield, which had sent Sam on numerous international assignments. The company asked Sam to represent them in Israel, where they legally sold state of the art equipment to support that nation's military preparedness. It was while he was in Israel that Sam ran into trouble for the first time. An Israeli patriot, Matti Stein, devastated by still another violent attack from Gaza, asked Sam to provide equipment not as yet allowed by our country. Sam is Jewish, but is an American first. He had long raised money for the Federation of Jewish Philanthropies, bought Israeli bonds and encouraged his friends to do the same. But he also regularly contributed to United Way, to his own and his children's universities, to the Sea Cliff Fire Department and to animal rescue and environmental causes.

"Matti Stein convinced Samuel Marcus to break the law for the first time. We acknowledge that Sam had long disagreed with U.S. policy toward Israel, which involved the withholding of certain weapon systems. Sam felt these items were crucial for Israel's defense. He used his contacts in the United States to obtain the needed equipment. It is important for you jurors to know that the U.S. changed its policy, and now supplies these and other more sophisticated systems to Israel. (Carlos took a short pause here, my guess, to allow the jurors to take in this point.)

"You may legitimately wonder, if Sam Marcus was such a patriot, why he benefited financially from these illegal transactions. You will learn from family friends and others why Sam Marcus felt he needed more money than he could earn legally, and why he couldn't share this with his wife and adult children. Now, do these realities justify his actions? We don't claim so. Sam Marcus does not claim this. He deeply regrets some of what he felt he had to do at that time."

Your father's gaze was unwavering in his focus on

the judge. In an hushed courtroom, Carlos continued: "We will show you how, following Sam's indiscretions, he was hunted by the enemies of Israel, blackmailed, his life and the lives of those he loved threatened. To diminish their vulnerability, he chose a path against his own values, expanding his illegal activities to other countries. Please withhold judgment until you have all the facts. And thank you for your intelligent attention and patience."

Carlos joined the Marcus family in mother's apartment. We were amazed at how energetic he appeared after this rough day.

"Mrs. Marcus, Rhoda, I hope your kids are being kind to you. This is torture for the strongest among us." Carlos put his arm around my mother after moving his chair closer to hers. He whispered, "From tomorrow on, when the prosecution is presenting their witnesses, you're gonna hear things that will disturb – even horrify you. You shouldn't feel that you must be there throughout the trial."

Mother responded to his warmth, saying "I really appreciate how concerned you are for me. Sally made a good decision asking you to defend Sam." She looked at me, reached out her hand to grab mine, adding, "I have to be in court. How would it look to the jury if Sam's wife wasn't there to support him? And what would I do with myself all day, wondering what was going on?"

Larry joined us in time for dinner. His demeanor matched his words: "Mom, you owe dad nothing! I saw you using your blood pressure machine after court yesterday. What did it read? That's been the case since his return. That man abused you, humiliated you, now will kill you. Is that what you want? Remember your grandchildren, even if you don't give a damn about yourself or us.

Following her husband's tirade, Elisa responded, calmly: "Larry, look at me! You shouldn't be trying to work gigs nights and be in court days. Impossible for any human, worse for someone with your temperament." Chuckling, Elisa pretended to cover Larry's mouth; then, arm embracing him, she tenderly escorted Larry out of the dining room. He pretended to resist, but his wide grin outed him.

Before leaving, Carlos, back against the door, planted a kiss on my forehead, then locked eyes with mine with a message he demanded I receive. I had to fight against an urge to leave with him.

My mother and I were both exhausted but unable to sleep, so converged after midnight in the kitchen to have one of our friendlier conversations.

"Sally, I have the impression that Carlos cares for you – beyond friendship. Elisa noticed that he hardly takes his eyes off you, pays attention to your every word. Not that he ignores us – I'm not complaining. He's a gentleman."

"There was once a lot of chemistry between us, mom. You know that. But we only were together for a few months before he dumped me. That whole time he was confused about us, about his life. He minimized his own strengths, intelligence, drive, while I thought then that he exaggerated how easy the rest of us had it. Now that he's successful, he's free to be himself. That doesn't mean he and I are back to where we were before we split. We're older, both have been in other relationships, and had plenty of life challenges to deal with."

"You're just out of a serious relationship, my smart daughter. Don't jump into another. But I am proud of you – unlike me, you were able to get out when you knew it was wrong for you."

"Don't compliment me, Mom. Jonah was the stronger one. Anger and disappointment propelled him to take action to protect himself. Thankfully, we were both able to get past the bad stuff, to reclaim some of our affection for each other on his birthday weekend. And Jonah and I get what you're saying, that we're not to be lovers, that's over. But we may be able to be friends in the not near future.

"I have plenty on my plate with dad's mess. And Jonah realizes that while he thought he had recovered from his wife's death, that there's more for him to work through. We both can use good shrinks!"

When mom nodded at this, then added, "For that you need a job,"

I was sure she's tired of being my bank account, seeing her own holdings diminished. Wow, I admire that. But it does put pressure on me at a time I can hardly handle anything else.

———————

"Sally, where are you? I looked for you after court. You and your mother took off. I didn't even get a chance to tell you how composed you were on the stand. Bravo! Are you both okay?"

"Yeah, we're good. I'm exhausted – emotionally, but all this sitting isn't doing me much good. I'm in mom's apartment, changing to workout clothes – headed to Central Park for a run."

"How about I join you? Say in an hour? We can clean up afterward in my hotel room, and head out to dinner."

We found each other on 59th Street and Fifth Avenue, a remarkable feat in the midst of unimaginable crowds. Observing that Europe and Asia must have emptied out, we slowly entered the park, watching out for the bicyclists and runners, as well as for other couples pushing baby carriages. Was this a good idea? Not so sure. But once we started jogging on a less trafficked trail, it became fun. The weather wasn't ideal, chilly, though not cold, a stiff, intermittent headwind limiting speed. Shifting from a modest jog to running warmed us. As we arrived closer to our agreed upon end point, I began my usual obsessing. Would I go to his room? Admitting to myself, yes, I want to go, but…

Carlos propelled me out of the park and into the downtown subway, heading to the Millennium Hilton. What I imagined would happen did. Entering his suite, he began kissing me, my lips, my neck down to my taut nipples, before letting me go momentarily to undress. Smiling broadly, he motioned me to do the same. When we were both nude, admiring each other's tight bodies, he lifted me up - our lips holding, to carry me into the immaculate bathroom. In the shower, Carlos caressed me with gel on my breasts, between my legs. I reciprocated before tasting him. His taut penis entered me, my legs around his waist. I hadn't been this aroused since he and I made love years before. When he came and exited my body, Carlos kissed me with intensity, before wrapping me in a marvelous pure white Egyptian bath towel. He ripped the coverlet off the king-sized bed, its purity soon to be despoiled by our lovemaking. A short nap followed by iced peach Secco left us both starving, and me thoughtful.

I wanted to convince myself this was just sex – as in the past, great sex. While we both dressed so that we could order room service, I wasn't so sure. Even he seemed less in command of words. My anxiety spiked. I silently prayed that I wasn't falling in love with him again.

Carlos had ordered dinner for both of us; though it was tasty and attractively presented, neither of us ate much. The waiter who later came to retrieve our plates inquired if we were unhappy with the fare.

I was ready to leave, but Carlos insisted we must talk.

"Sally, I could flatter you by saying that I always loved you and waited for this moment. But you're too smart to believe that, and I suck at lying to someone I care about. How good is a lawyer who can't lie, huh?" We both grinned.

I succeeded in overcoming unaccustomed shyness to be as honest as he was: "I am very nervous around you, Carlos. I think it's because in spite of my relationship with Jonah, I've often had fantasies of our being together someday, after we met at conferences. I am attracted to you, physically and intellectually. But years ago, you were so distant. Can I trust how you'd different be if we were to try again?"

"Look, I won't defend my old behavior. You knew it was a rotten time for me. And I didn't trust that we could talk about serious issues, like my being of mixed-race; what would that mean to you - and to your family - if we did ever marry. In spite of my being in love with you – there, I said it – I had to move on. And you were Jewish." He laughed, but the humor was lost on me. I wondered, is he anti-Semitic?

"I'm still Jewish."

"Yes, but these days. so are many of my closest friends and colleagues. And I am no longer a practicing Catholic, to my mother's horror."

"You've had girlfriends. Were they gorgeous, smart, Catholic, Hispanic?"

"Yes, one fit the bill perfectly. We lived together

for two years, and I would have married her. Except she was never around. She had – has – a passion for her career. She's a nature photographer, spends most of her life in Africa. Our relationship was heavy with WattsApp and emails. A year ago, we agreed to split. I was pretty bummed for a few months. But my work as usual rescued me."

Carlos took a bathroom break. I had decided to leave, but waited for his return. Seeing me standing, jacket on, ready for our goodbyes, he pulled me into a bear hug. "I want for us to have a second chance. Let's not blow it." I couldn't help noticing that we both had tears about to descend. Nodding after his gentle kiss, I left.

I had decided to take the subway uptown to mom's, but couldn't quite force myself to deal with the high-paced anonymous crowds heading down the subway stairs at this hour. It was only 8:30, dark and windy, more than chilly. I worried - could someone be following me? While I tried to talk myself out of that notion, McMahon's words Be Careful! won out. On Broadway I managed to catch an uptown taxi. Then, on impulse - a familiar driver of my behavior these days, I had him pull over once we were in the Village, this after staring at the rapidly accelerating meter. I cannot afford the projected $50 tariff.

For over an hour, I wandered around small familiar shops with no intention of buying anything. I refused to allow myself to think - not about Carlos, not about dad's situation, not about my vulnerability. On entering a familiar nail salon open at this late hour, I focused on the choice of colors for a gel manicure, which I also couldn't afford.

CHAPTER 23

W hile alone with my father on Saturday morning, he asked me if I knew that "… my old friends are turning against me. But I can hardly blame them. Your mother had the right to be miserable with me, to talk to her friends. I gave her plenty of grief, reasons to hate me. Hell, even you and Larry were in on the act. How come you don't hate me?"

"At times I did. I remember seeing Adele's father, Dr. Joe, and wishing he were my dad, that her mom was my mom. I wanted a family where parents liked each other, loved each other, instead of fighting whenever they had to be together. Especially once Larry left, it was bad. I heard the screaming from your bedroom. Yes, sometimes I hated you both."

"Well, kid, you certainly don't pull your punches. That wasn't you as a little girl. You looked up to me, wanted to be with me. I remember you begging me to take you on the boat even on nasty days when all I was gonna do was clean it."

"Yeah, that's true. You were the more interesting parent, with fascinating tales of far-off places, the one who brought me exotic dolls, who taught me chess and encouraged my riding and tennis. And mom didn't seem to like me. Eventually, I came to understand that I had to pay a price with you: do what you enjoyed, or you lost interest in me. By the time I was at Barnard, that choice had lost its luster."

"You're making me sound like a self-indulgent son-of-a-bitch. Maybe I was. But I'll tell you something. If I had been happier with your mother, I'd have been a different man."

"You can't blame her for who you were. That might have worked for you when I was a kid, but the adult I am demands more honesty from you. Then again, you never tolerated what you didn't want to hear."

We lapsed into an uncomfortable silence, caught up in our own memories. Out of the blue, he jumped up, walked across to where I remained seated, and pulled me to my feet with a bear hug. It lasted a long time. His parting words: "When this is over, Sally, if I get out of here alive, I will be different. Hold me to it!

The prosecution's case had been proceeding well for them. We might have been devastated as the evidence unfolded except for Carlos' frequent warning: "Just because they say it's true, doesn't make it so." Watching his cross-examination also helped. He is a master at creating doubt, emphasizing that many of the witnesses had their own agenda, their own checkered pasts.

My own testimony, which had followed my interrogation by the assistant prosecutor, had been limited to my role in bringing dad into custody. Until helping the FBI locate him, I had no knowledge of my father's whereabouts since last seeing him years before on campus.

Ms. Leland's testimony covered most of the years of dad's supposed crimes and therefore would be difficult for the defense to dispute. She was a credible witness, at the outset acknowledging her own conflict: she still loved Sam Marcus, thus had a wish to protect him, and yet had a strong commitment to the truth.

Leland stated: "My friend and lover, Sam Marcus, initially spent a lot of time with me in London. We vacationed in Barcelona and Israel on two separate occasions. Until approximately two years ago, he told me nothing of why he had begun so much travelling, and why his calls to me had become infrequent during the previous six months. Even before he shared his trouble, I had an inkling that something wasn't right. He wasn't well – hypertension– unexplained loss of appetite and weight loss, and he didn't sleep peacefully when he was with me. He was distractible, lost interest in going with me to museums or the theatre, which he had previously enjoyed. Of course I was worried, and asked him what was troubling him; getting no response, I dropped it."

The lead prosecutor asked additional questions about their life together prior to Sam coming clean with Ms. Leland, then shifted to what she had been told of his criminal activities.

"Specifically, Ms. Leland, what did Samuel Marcus tell you about what he was up to? Tell us when those conversations occurred. Keep in mind your own vulnerability to prosecution, should you dissemble."

"Sam admitted that he was in legal trouble. That he had brought in shipments of small machinery and computer guidance programs to several countries in the Middle East. He was ashamed, he said, of helping any country except Israel. He was firm in telling me not to ask him for details, worried that I could be seen as an accomplice, should he be apprehended. So I do not know anything more, beyond that on rare occasions when I saw him or spoke to him in the months before his capture, he did say that others were after him. That if he failed to contact me again, it wasn't because he had stopped caring for me."

After this comment, she appeared to be on the verge of collapse. The Judge gave her time to collect herself, calling a recess. When court resumed, the prosecutor asked a few more questions, which had previously been answered, and Carlos gently cross-examined. Nothing new emerged, beyond her acknowledging that she had visited dad in prison prior to her being refused entry. And she volunteered that she had every intention of seeing him now that she had testified, and that she forgave him, and would continue being his friend.

The witness we were most concerned about, Matti Stein, took the stand. To my eyes, he was almost too self-assured, verging on cocky. He smiled at Miri, who had again traveled from Israel to lend her support. Following the usual questions (name, address, country of birth, occupation, marital status,) the real interrogation began:

"What was your involvement, beyond your

legitimate activities as a self-employed accountant, in Israel prior to meeting the defendant?"

"I raised money for some people who were trying to help Israel."

"Please be specific. From whom did you seek money? For what purposes?"

"Mainly from Jewish Americans. Some French and English. Israel has lobbyists in Washington seeking the U.S. Congress' support for our military – they have to be above board. Not so us. We could reach out to our friends under the radar, to do more. They generally did."

"Exactly what did they do? You said they raised money. How much? For what?"

"Well, I can't say how much because I wasn't the only one involved on our end. Bt it was hundreds of millions of dollars. The money went for equipment, information, software that we wanted but couldn't get any other way. I just filled orders – didn't know much about the stuff."

"Who in the Israeli government knew about this clandestine activity?"

"I never knew. I didn't want to know. Whoever it was, they didn't want me to know. We copied a system from the French underground during World War II, layered, each group reporting to someone above him. The guy I dealt with committed suicide five years ago."

"His name?" For the first time, Stein's cockiness took a hit.

"Aaron Maisel. He was from Toronto, had immigrated to Israel with his family as a teenager. He

served in our military. After the Air Force, he went
to McGill in Montreal. For aeronautical engineering.
He returned to the Technion for his Ph.D. Aaron
understood first hand what the military needed, and
he tried his best to help get it. A real patriot."

"All right. Tell us what projects you were directly
involved in at the point you encountered Sam Marcus.
How did you meet him?"

"We met socially, through his friend, my sister,
Batya. Sam Marcus had fathered a child with her while
she was his student at Cooper Union in New York.
When Sam first came to meet Miri, their child, Batya
introduced us. He had come to Israel for his son's Bar
Mitzvah."

"Before you and Marcus began to collaborate on
illegal efforts, what did you know of his prior activities?"

Carlos objected – hearsay. Sustained.

"Mr. Stein, what did you and Mr. Marcus discuss on
the occasion you entertained your first joint venture?"

"We discussed our philosophies, our take on what
Israel's vulnerability was, her politics, 'cause there was
a growing, strong liberal faction in both countries crazy
enough to believe that the Palestinians really wanted
peace."

Before Mrs. Anderson could ask her next question,
Matti Stein jumped in to add: "Lots of us were wary of
your country's ideas way back, since President Carter,
and didn't trust Obama either. We thought he was naïve,
at best, dealing with Iran. Trump's ok, on our team."

When court resumed, Stein reported, in remarkable

detail, conversations he had had with dad years before. These had focused on requests for specific items, with dad's filling Stein in on his efforts to acquire them. Carlos' intermittent objections were mostly overruled. Stein shared information that truly shocked us: Dad had acquired a Smith & Wesson .357 Magnum via Stein. This weapon had been found in dad's possession when he was arrested. I hadn't known that.

Placed into evidence was Stein's handwritten, dated list of money transactions following dad's delivery of requested items. Stein had not handled any money himself and denied being paid off to do what he did. He just authorized the money transfers. He ended his testimony with sarcasm: "Israelis don't have to be paid to be patriots!"

I glanced at my father several times during Stein's testimony. He seemed detached. Mother and I shared our concern that his demeanor might repel the jury.

Days later, Ben Fisher took the stand. Unlike Stein, Mr. Fisher appeared fearful, almost ill. His natural healthy complexion had shifted to gray, accentuated by his gray suit and white shirt. He couldn't hide his long, shaking legs, which he crossed and uncrossed throughout his testimony. The poor man had a tic over his tearing right eye.

Mom and I compared our thoughts about these two very different men. Stein, who was a player, lied whenever he felt the need, but came across as sincere; Fisher, whom we both knew to be the most ethical of this motley crew, told the truth, yet evoked suspicion. So much for observation promoting accurate conclusions.

Ben Fisher went over some basic information with Mrs. Anderson before she zeroed in on what she wanted to know. "When and under what circumstances did you and Sam Marcus meet, and when did he invite you to join him in a criminal enterprise?"

Though Carlos objected to her wording, she was able to get what she needed.

"Sam and I met when our daughters were young, and again when the girls went to camp together. We might have chatted about business. He urged me to buy Israel bonds; I bought them at my brokerage firm.

"My trouble began when the girls were in high school. They were friends, both applying to Barnard. It's very expensive. I had put aside the tuition, but my wife was diagnosed with metastatic breast cancer. Health insurance paid 70% - I had to come up with $140,000, for chemo, radiation, the mastectomy. I went through everything we had, even maxed out our credit cards. I never told my wife. And I was too much the coward to tell my daughter she had to go to Brooklyn or Queens College. They're much less expensive, and just as good.

"I saw Sam Marcus at a Jewish Federation dinner meeting during the worst time, and spilled everything. He was sympathetic. The following weekend he and Rhoda – his wife – took us to Peter Luger's for steak dinner to celebrate a deal Sam had concluded. Days later, he offered me what he called a partnership. I'm ashamed to say I grabbed it."

"What were the terms of this so-called partnership?"

"Sam knew I was – am – a CPA. He asked me to handle the books for what he called his private enterprise. For great pay. I'd be lying if I said that I wasn't suspicious right away. I didn't want to know much. Later, when I understood more clearly, I wanted out. Sam said no way, we're in too deep. I believed him. By then I knew others had to be involved – though I never met most of them. I authorized payments for different people. Sam told me the guys had to do with shipments to Israel."

"You want this jury to believe that's all you knew?"

"Of course I understood the airport people flew cargo to Tel Aviv. But I never had the full picture 'til the FBI began questioning me. I'm sure that's the way Sam wanted it. After I moved to Tel Aviv, Sam and I met once. I refused to continue, and he didn't push the issue. I didn't need the money anymore. Besides, I was more scared of the Israeli police than of Sam. It didn't occur to me then that the FBI was involved." Retreating for a time, Ben Fisher seemed drained. But he added: "I sound stupid even to myself."

Over the next two weeks, the aforementioned airline pilots and handlers testified. The lead prosecutor tried to put into evidence sworn statements from a few of dad's former Israeli colleagues, but Carlos objected, not having access to questioning them. The Judge upheld his objection.

On resting their case, both prosecutors looked positively buoyant. They had the option of reopening if and when those 'colleagues' could testify in person. Cleared of jury and spectators, the Judge authorized a one week adjournment to allow the attorneys to travel to Israel to examine these men, both of whom were in custody.

The prisoners had been separated for interrogation, each with his attorney. Both testified that they met Samuel Marcus through Matti Stein, for whom they had done prior work. On one occasion, they met a man who was handling their payments. Both men stated that several times - they couldn't be more specific - they drove a rented truck to a private airport south of Tel Aviv to pick up merchandise. They never knew what was in the containers – of varying sizes – but had been told by telephone that the packages contained 'highly classified' material. One of the men testified that he hadn't known what 'highly classified' meant, but never inquired. His only interest was the money, received after delivery to a previously designated warehouse. Both men acknowledged that they knew what they were doing was illegal. Their total income over the four year period: $22,000 each, paid in dollars. Of course they did not pay income tax on the funds; both men had been warned not to spend their windfall in an obvious way. They complied.

These men, seen on tape in court a week after interrogation, might have been older editions of those I saw meeting with my father at the King David Hotel that summer I worked as a counselor. What if I, then fifteen, had had the courage to ask dad more pointed questions?

Could I have saved him from disaster? Ridiculous to imagine that a kid – especially the kid I was – could have made that impact.

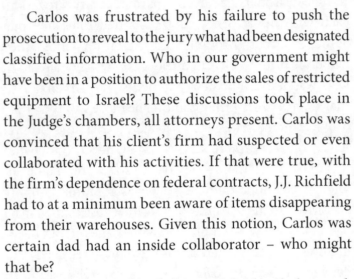

Carlos was frustrated by his failure to push the prosecution to reveal to the jury what had been designated classified information. Who in our government might have been in a position to authorize the sales of restricted equipment to Israel? These discussions took place in the Judge's chambers, all attorneys present. Carlos was convinced that his client's firm had suspected or even collaborated with his activities. If that were true, with the firm's dependence on federal contracts, J.J. Richfield had to at a minimum been aware of items disappearing from their warehouses. Given this notion, Carlos was certain dad had an inside collaborator – who might that be?

The former President of J.J. Richfield took the stand. That distinguished 74 year old gentleman presented as most cooperative, even jovial, in initial questioning. After preliminary inquiries, Carlos got tougher.

"Mr. Lane, you acknowledged that your V.P/ Director of international sales did inquire of you as to why Sam Marcus was authorized to make trips abroad during the years in question, as the firm had specific staff members for such activities. Did you personally authorize the trips?"

"No, I did not. But I supported the company's

CFO, who had recommended them. We had reviewed both expenditures and results of our new efforts in the Middle East. Sam Marcus had been sent to Israel because he spoke conversational Hebrew and had excellent contacts within the business community. We greatly benefitted from his expertise in the area."

"Were you aware of his trips to Egypt, Morocco, Spain, Kuwait?"

"Yes to Egypt, Morocco, Kuwait and Bahrain. To my knowledge, Spain was never authorized." After a pause, he added: "Dale Young informed me that Sam might consider a transfer to our international division. If that were the case, and he made a formal request, it would have posed a challenge, in that his foreign activities had reduced his availability for domestic sales, and we had no one ready to move into his position. In anticipation of that problem, we asked Sam to begin working with his associate, to ready that man for promotion in the event Sam elected to formalize the change."

"Were there accounting and other measures in place at that time to reveal problems with missing or misplaced equipment?"

"Of course, we had careful monitoring, financially and otherwise. Nothing of value was reported missing during my tenure. If I recall correctly, from time to time an item was misplaced or mislabeled, only to be located in one of our warehouses in Washington State or Texas."

"Now, Mr. Lane, you told us, and we verified, that Dale Young died 2.6 years ago, while still on the job. That timing is particularly of interest because it coincides precisely with Mr. Marcus' retirement from participation in his illegal business activities abroad. Company records which have been produced to us showed nothing untoward. Do you have personal knowledge of any private transactions which Mr. Young might have conducted with Sam Marcus, following Mr. Marcus' retirement from J.J. Richfield, five years ago?"

"Certainly not! Sounding irritated for the first time, Mr. Lane began to fidget. "Remember, I'm retired over three years."

Carlos saw an opening here, but elected to ask the witness to step down, with the option of recalling him at a later date. Judge Marianna Costello adjourned the morning session.

Without a word to Sally and her family, Carlos and his co-counsel left the area. On their return, without explanation, Judge Costello adjourned court for the day.

I had left a message for Carlos, anxious to find out what had come up to cause this unexpected adjournment; he did not return my call. Tense, imagining something exciting was in the works, to provide a welcome distraction mom treated Elisa and me to massages and facials. Afterward, avoiding aimless chatter about the trial, we three strolled through Greenwich Village on this beautiful Spring day, visiting dress shops and noshing on delicious tacos from a local street vendor.

All the key players reassembled in court the following morning. Carlos called his first witness: Ms. Ellen Fuchs. After preliminaries, Ms. Fuchs identified herself as having been Dale Young's private secretary at J.J. Richfield until his untimely death.

"Ms. Fuchs, you worked for Mr. Young for approximately eight years, until his death some 2 ½ years ago?"

"Yes, sir."

"Do you still work for J.J. Richfield?"

"No, sir. I got married over three years ago. We live in Connecticut, so it was a big trip for me. After Mr. Young's death, I resigned." She smiled to herself at some private thought "I have a baby now, so I don't work."

"Congratulations. That's wonderful. Please turn your attention to your years of working closely with Mr. Young. Do you recall instances when things went missing? Where you were asked to do anything out of the ordinary about that?"

Ms. Fuchs did not respond with her previous alacrity. "Yes, I guess so. When I asked about some item – only a few here and there – Mr. Young would say another department had taken responsibility for it. I'm very orderly. So I wanted to be able to put down in my records which department, but Mr. Young would always say he'd get back to me on that later."

"Did he?"

"No. After a few times, I got the message. So I didn't ask anymore."

"What did you think was going on?"

Objection from the prosecution sustained.

"Ms. Fuchs, did you pursue the question about the missing items with anyone else in the company?"

"No, never. I didn't want to think that anything was wrong. Mr. Young and I had worked together for a long time. I was very fond of him. He treated me great, with respect. Always recommended me for merit increases. I wanted to believe that he was doing good for the company, maybe something secret for our government."

"Wouldn't Mr. Young have told you that? Surely at other times he did."

"Yes."

"To your knowledge, did Mr. Young and the defendant have contact during the years following Mr. Marcus' retirement from J.J. Richfield?"

"Not in person, so far as I know. But they talked on the telephone. They had been friends for a long time. Mr. Young told me that Sam Marcus was having the time of his life in retirement, living abroad. That he – Dale that is, would one day also become a 'bon vivant'. His words. Dale also gave me regards from Mr. Marcus."

"Did you ever listen in on any of these telephone calls?"

"Of course not!" She added: "The calls came in on

Mr. Young's cell phone, not the company's lines." At this, Ms. Fuchs' started to look like a woman having a hot flash, red to her ears, sweaty, her eyes darting from the defendant to Carlos.

"You appear distressed, Ms. Fuchs. Please share with the court what thoughts produced your discomfort."

"I just realized that something may have been going on with them. I swear, I never thought it then. I don't know anything more." With that, the witness began sobbing: "Oh, my God, I always thought Mr. Young was so wonderful."

"Did you have a private, intimate relationship with him?"

She nodded. "Yes. He was divorced. I wasn't married then. We didn't do anything wrong."

"Certainly not. What do you know about his death? We have gotten conflicting statements on this – that he had a heart attack while on a vacation abroad. That he died following a skiing accident."

"Dale was killed skiing in Switzerland. Swiss authorities sent a report to the company. It said that Dale was found midway on an off-trail slope used by their ski patrol and by the Swiss Olympic team. I was shocked. He was an excellent skier, but always said skiing past your skill level was foolish and dangerous. He was very critical of that Kennedy fellow who died after crashing into a tree while playing football on an advanced slope."

"The medical examiner report stated that Dale had

probably suffered a coronary before the accident. Were you aware of his having any heart problems?"

"No. As far as I knew, he was very healthy. He jogged, swam. He was always encouraging me to be more active. He loved to dance. So do I."

"At the time, were you suspicious as to the cause of his death?"

Before Ms. Fuchs could respond, the prosecution objected - but not before the jury got the message. Mr. Young, the defendant's likely partner, may have been murdered.

Carlos called J.J. Richfield's former President Elliot Lane back to the stand. This time, Mr. Lane did not look at all jovial. Carlos was now able to use information gathered from Ms. Fuchs' testimony to explore Mr. Lane's knowledge of Dale Young's behavior on the job.

"Were you aware that certain things had gone missing under Mr. Young's watch? Things that were not ever located."

"Of course not. I already told you as much."

"Were you aware of Mr. Young's ongoing relationship with the defendant, and his use of his cell phone to communicate about machinery with Mr. Marcus?"

"I never asked Dale what phone he used to talk with Sam. They were friends. At times Dale sent Sam's regards to me after their chats. Did I know what they talked about? Why would I? The answer is NO!"

Carlos called a number of other witnesses, some of whom testified to his client's devoted service to his country, his on-site trainings with the armed services on their use of new complex equipment. Other character witnesses spoke of Marcus' generosity to charities ranging from his local fire department, various universities, Hadassah and Jewish Federation. A few long-standing friends, those less critical of Marcus' extra-marital behavior, also testified on his behalf.

CHAPTER 24

Carlos and I, both drained, dealt with the end of the trial by again going to his hotel, supposedly for drinks. At the time, I had no conscious intent to go to his room. But drinks morphed into dinner in the hotel's stunning intimate restaurant; we became each other's desert.

What a difference a few years make. I was no longer the worshipful twenty year old; he wasn't the uptight, self-conscious poor Mexican. We avoided serious conversation about any future between us, taking pleasure in our mutual attraction. And, this time we could laugh together at our younger uptight selves.

Nevertheless, hours later, an irrational guilt attacked me, as if I had betrayed Jonah. Weird me.

But actual trouble happened when I returned to mom's condo. She had waited up for her 25 year old-daughter! Acting the part of "poor" Jonah's defender, she laced into me: "What kind of a woman are you? You lived with a man who you supposedly loved, who loved you, then leave for a few months to think about your relationship – and jump into bed, just like that, with an old flame!"

I did not take kindly to her diatribe. At 2 am, I taxied over to Aunt Lily's. She welcomed me, no questions asked. In the morning, we conferred on why mom might not want me with Carlos. From my astute aunt: "She doesn't dislike him. But he's not Jewish. He's a Mexican living in California. (I interpreted: not white) - "...she hopes you will stay in New York for good. She's disappointed that you and Jonah are finished, imagined that he'd move here for you." That would not have happened.

I was equally candid. "Guess what? Carlos and I are nowhere near being serious about our relationship. But if and when I do marry, religion is irrelevant to me. And I am far from deciding where to live. I must find a job, and soon. Maybe because mom has been helping me with money, she thinks she can treat me like an adolescent again."

From Aunt Lily: "Healthy on all counts! Your acknowledging how you have always needed a guy in your life, how that sometimes meant you were hasty in your choices - that's real growth. Here's to giving our shrinks credit."

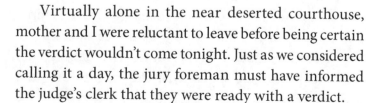

Virtually alone in the near deserted courthouse, mother and I were reluctant to leave before being certain the verdict wouldn't come tonight. Just as we considered calling it a day, the jury foreman must have informed the judge's clerk that they were ready with a verdict.

It took over an hour for all parties to be located. Dad, pale, too thin, showed no emotion at this life-changing event. Carlos, by his side, arm on dad's shoulder, was whispering to him. The lead prosecutor, Mrs. Anderson, sat alone, her co-counsel not yet located. We all awaited the Judge. When she arrived, I turned to make eye contact with my mother. She looked away. We were out of words, stiffened by fear.

Judge Costello emerged, requesting that the clerk escort the jurors into the courtroom. Seven men and five women, all looking grave, several appearing exhausted, entered behind their foreman, a slim African-American middle-aged man. The jurors never looked at dad. A bad sign? Judge Costello read the charges. All eyes shifted from her to the jury's foreman as he rose to report the verdict.

Multiple shots exploded from the back of the courtroom. Shifting my eyes from behind us to my dad, I ran to him, bulldozing my way past mother. It never occurred to me that we might be killed. Jurors were herded out of the courtroom. Someone must have escorted Judge Costello, the prosecutors and the court reporter to safety, but I did not notice. I saw only dad, face down on the table, with Carlos beside him.

I later learned that the one guard stationed at the entrance to the courtroom had been shot from behind, never having drawn his weapon. The killer had escaped.

Mother joined me, screaming, touching her husband – her bloody hand on the back of his head testimony to his state. Inexplicably, she asked me, "Is he dead? I can't believe that." I pulled her away, too forcefully, I think. Another bullet had grazed Carlos' left shoulder. He tried to say something to us – but his own pain and the arrival of EMT to take both dad and Carlos to a nearby hospital cut off our words. The stench of blood and of my own sweat left me dizzy, faint. Mother and I leaned against the defense table, immobilized, until the police appeared to escort us and others, including the excited media, out of the courthouse.

I didn't know what to do with myself. I must stay with mom. Should we follow the ambulance to the hospital? Larry appeared before I even called him, having heard the news while in a nearby hotel. Seeing the shape we both were in, he shoved mom and me into a cab.

Hours later, Carlos called. He had been treated and released from Beth Israel Hospital. It was only after I knew he was well that I collapsed. Dad, close to death on arrival, was in surgery.

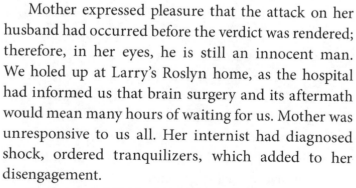

Mother expressed pleasure that the attack on her husband had occurred before the verdict was rendered; therefore, in her eyes, he is still an innocent man. We holed up at Larry's Roslyn home, as the hospital had informed us that brain surgery and its aftermath would mean many hours of waiting for us. Mother was unresponsive to us all. Her internist had diagnosed shock, ordered tranquilizers, which added to her disengagement.

Devastated, Miri had flown in to be with us. Mother

insisted that she not be introduced to our visitors as family, a decision Larry and I agreed not to challenge. Eliza was warm in her welcome to Miri, and in her role as hostess to the many who came. She still needed to attend her children. Isabel was tearful, looking for answers, while Matthew generally remained in his room, except for meals.

People – mobs to my mind – descended, some caring, others, I'm sure, curious. They sent food, cakes, flowers, contributed to charities. Many were not known to me, new friends of mom's, colleagues of Larry's. A few of our old neighbors arrived, as did several of my Barnard friends.

The media sensationalized our lives, shifting this private tragedy into a made-for-movies drama. For days, we were too numb to care. But soon, I traversed from numb to rage, and was at times barely civil.

A quieter, devastated Carlos was a fixture those first few days, I believe in shock himself. He then flew home to take back his life. On departure day, hugging me, he admitted feeling "...on the margins responsible for your father's attack," before asking me to promise that we'd get together soon in California.

Elisa wondered why I hadn't told my Chicago friends about dad's condition. While I was staying with her, she was free to ask questions she must have been curious about for years. "I have no close friends there, only acquaintances, Jonah's friends." Afterward, I added, "I never got involved with anyone at work either. We were so busy, then I was gone more than there. I've never been good keeping women friends. Even at Stanford, where I had the warmest study mates and other girls I socialized with, I never shared our family's troubles. I was ashamed. And haven't kept in touch, even after they reached out to me."

"Sally, you were so welcoming to me from the start. I think of you as my sister, my best friend – and that was soon after we moved here. I so missed you when you left. And you know that Larry and I have put you in our will as our children's guardians, should anything happen to us."

She paused, then added: "Aren't you lonely, not having close friends?"

"Lonely? Yeah, though I don't often let myself acknowledge that, even to myself. Once dad vanished, my life outside of school, then work, was peculiar, shifting from obsession about him, to blocking out the whole mess. My own crazy mental state didn't really allow anyone in, including Jonah. Did I use Jonah? Maybe. He cared for me when I hadn't a clue what I would do with my life. He took over, providing shelter, people, activities. I let him. We might have gone on like that except for dad's return. But maybe not. Jonah was tiring of me."

Elisa averted her gaze, then rose to get us some wine. On her return, I shared my truth: "I'm a terrible person. A user. Now you know how messed up I am. Maybe I am just like my dad – I can appear warm and interested. When I do stick out relationships, I become needy, demanding. Watch out! You could become another victim." Elisa reached out with a hug. She seemed near tears, shook her head in denial of what I had said.

"I'm horrified that you would think that about yourself. Most of us are in and out about trusting others, especially in your family situation. I began to distrust Larry soon after we moved here. He was so different, not all of it explainable by your father's behavior – even before he disappeared. Would you believe that I secretly made plans to leave with Isabel – I was so depressed. Instead, Larry and I went to counseling; that got us back. Larry relaxed. My depression lifted. We became a family again.

"Sally, we figured it out together. We healed in that talking. We understood how your family's rotating around your father, his comings and goings, his successes, his infidelities, his presents, all left no air for anyone else. In that family your mother didn't exist. Larry didn't feel he mattered until he left for Oberlin; and you, my darling sister, do you recall telling me that Barnard was your first real home?"

"Yeah, I said that. Why then didn't I keep in touch with friends I made there? Like Ginger, who I loved and respected – but resented when she transferred to Juilliard. Getting a man to love me was always my number one objective. I never met anyone fitting that description while I was in college. When I became good friends with a girl, I'd ditch her in a heartbeat if a boy I liked appeared on the scene." Elisa, biting her lower lip, seemed momentarily speechless, likely reluctant to say more. But she couldn't contain herself: "Sal, in whatever way you feel yourself to be unhealthy, you can change. Look what you've already gotten past – lifelong rejection from your mom, your dad's behavior, even sexual abuse. Please, please believe in yourself."

"I'm working on it, 'Lisa, dear. Not easy… but I can't tell you how much you're helping me, my precious sister." My tears became a flood with sound effects, soon joined by Elisa's. She grabbed me: "I love you. We, Larry, our kids, Aunt Lily, even your mom, we all adore you. Feast on our love, draw from it. Let us nourish you"

Carlos and I spoke briefly on several occasions over the next few days. After the 'how are you,' there wasn't much more to say, beyond sharing news; there was none about dad. I never asked if he still felt guilty about dad's assault, and knew from my own silent musings that I have been tempted to blame him. Had he checked on security? Everyone in that courtroom, after that horrific ending, had admitted noticing the reduced security. That included Carlos, the judge, and the media. Why hadn't mom and I noticed?

CHAPTER 25

Robin McMahon paid me an unexpected visit. His conveyed appreciation for my help, and inquired about those troubling calls, which thankfully, had ended. He then shifted gears:

"I'm here with some information I was sure you'd want to know. We had told you that your father and his attorney were attacked by a hired gunman. That man's prints were in the system. He had been here illegally from Egypt, and served time for gun possession six years ago, then was deported. Somehow, we're sure with help from locals, he got back into the states in time to do his job. We are looking into who helped him get back and then to gain access to the courtroom."

"So you don't have any new information."

"Not so fast. We don't have all the answers. But listen before you judge."

I could see that McMahon was trying to be helpful – so shut up. He continued: "We found barely legible notes, likely from the gunman's handlers, that Sam Marcus wouldn't rat on them so long as there was no death penalty issue. As the evidence piled up, they weren't so sure. After all, jurors seemed set to convict on all charges. The hired assassin couldn't chance waiting to see if your father was convicted – and if so, could be willing to trade information with the FBI. His bosses clearly did not know that NYS' highest court, in 2004 in People vs. LaValle, had declared the state's death penalty to be unconstitutional. Even inmates on death row had their sentences reduced to life in prison without the possibility of parole."

I stood up, intending to leave him alone in mom's living room. He stopped me. "Hear me out. When three years ago, after Dale Young's death, your father told the criminals he worked with that he could no longer produce, they did try to kill him. Remember that bomb scare in Cairo. That drove Sam Marcus into hiding. He told us of his suspicions they had killed Young, and was sure he'd be next. He was right. We got all this from your father after his arrest, during our first meeting in Bath. He denied being afraid for himself. His intent was to protect Alice, who had become the only person he trusted and loved. He didn't imagine that the Brotherhood could touch the family back home.

"Egypt has been cooperative to the extent of including us in the interrogations of the two guys implicated in terrorist activities there. These were the suspects in the bombing of an outdoor market, where dozens were killed or severely injured."

"You thought I wanted to hear more about what my father did?" I must have scowled at him, when I added: "Don't dare to tell my mother anything she hadn't already heard. She's still deluding herself that her husband was a patriot, doing what he believed was keeping Israel safe."

"Look, I'm here out of respect for you, for your

family, because there's no way that we can forever control what will come out. One day, maybe in months or even years, you will turn on the news, only to hear someone reporting more details on this sordid story. The days when we can control media are long gone. The Internet, social media, took care of that. I urge you to prepare your family."

Until McMahon showed up, I had begun to feel lighter. One night I even dreamed that I spent a lovely afternoon writing a poem for dad's headstone (killing him off before he died!). On awakening, I was momentarily elated, thinking he can't torture me anymore. This before guilt set in - dad's still unconscious, in fact being kept under heavy sedation following brain surgery. But he's not dead.

McMahon's visit upended me. I'll never be free. Who would want to hire me, with this history? I laughed at my naïvete, recalling my old fantasy of changing my name, how that would free me. Self pity took over, morphing to renewed worry about Matthew and Isabel. But not for long. I determined to embrace the very media that could undo us, reaching out to major outlets – CBS, NBC, Facebook, Twitter – to begin my attack.

Khaled Adiga's card was stuck outside my mailback when I returned to my studio rental ten days after McMahon's visit. The card identified him as FBI, listed a Manhattan telephone number, no address. He had handwritten: "Please contact me as soon as possible."

Larry had called to warn me: "Sis, you're getting a visitor – he just left my house. Another G-man. He's concerned for our safety. Quote: 'I don't want to alarm you, Mr. Marcus. We have no definite information, but we have some reason to believe that your family could be at risk.' When I asked why the devil anyone would be interested in us after dad was so close to death, he said my asking was nuts. I gave him your new address. Hope that's okay – but he'd get it anyway."

"Larry, I have a plan, but I don't want to talk about it over the phone. Call it paranoia, but I no longer trust even my cell phone. I can meet you tomorrow late afternoon – how about at Rockefeller Center?"

Khaled Adiga arrived at my door, having bypassed the doorman. When I looked through the peephole, he smiled, showing his badge. He did not fit my idea of FBI, much younger, early thirties, black hair worn past his ears, cocoa complexion, dressed casually in slacks topped by a yellow v-neck sweater, a blazer over his arm. He was 'cool.'

I let him into the foyer. After introductions, he made his way, without an invitation into the main room, saying "Nice place. I just heard from your brother that you had moved here. Good fortune to you." He actually motioned to me to sit on my couch. What nerve. Do they teach chutzpah in g-man school, or is he just a typical Middle Eastern man with a gene for controlling women?

"You are of course not pleased at my visit, but I am here to help, not to scare you. Your brother treated what I told him to be a joke. It's no joke, Ms. Marcus." (I must admit that he handled me pretty well, though at that moment, I was resentful.) "We are establishing more solid information on the killing of the guard, and the assaults on your father and his attorney. We how know how the killer gained access to the courtroom. We had presumed that he had waited during the trial, perhaps to see how it would progress, or he might have had trouble gaining entry before that evening. We had, after all, posted extra security.

"On that terrible occasion, the court supervisor cancelled security, believing that the jury would be retiring. The killer, or his accomplice, had surely been on surveillance for days, under our radar. When it was clear the jury was ready to report a verdict, poor Juan Rodriguez was called in as the sole security officer. We are now convinced that the killer was aided by an inside man who had previously smuggled in the weapon, and on this occasion, that man helped him to enter the courthouse. We are focused on fingering that insider."

"Are you just collecting a series of interesting hypotheses? Or do you expect to have someone in custody soon?"

"Look, I appreciate how upset you and your family are with law enforcement. You had helped capture your father to avoid his being killed. Naturally the idea of his being found guilty was distressing, but you imagined he'd be safe in federal prison. I'm so sorry, ma'am."

I didn't give a damn how sorry he felt. But I kept that to myself. I asked Adiga if he agreed with McMahon that our family was still in danger. "What could they imagine we knew that could harm them?"

"Good question, Ms. Marcus. The criminal cartel could believe that your father told or could eventually tell someone in the family – your mother, his brother, or his lawyer, who they are, where they train, how they fund their operations. The Muslim Brotherhood is extremely vulnerable in their home country, Egypt. They have upgraded training and weaponry, not for nothing, and have increasingly perpetrated terrorist attacks at home, possibly in collaboration with ISIS. Naturally, Egypt is committed to destroying both terrorist networks before they do even more damage to the country's economy. The US funds their army. So when we ask for help, they deliver, if they can."

"Carlos advised dad to avoid saying anything to any of us, and overall, he obeyed. We honored Carlos' request, never asking questions. How can we let the terrorists know that?"

"You want to talk to terrorists?" Now his grin widened. He was laughing at me. "You're are planning to go to the media. Guess what? They won't believe you. Your brother and his family are likely the most vulnerable, because of his celebrity. By the time he and I completed our discussion, his wife had returned home. She talked sense into her husband. He's now on board. The family is moving from their Manhasset home to a Manhattan rental, 24 hour doorman building – and they are transferring their children into a small private school."

"What should I do?"

"Stay where you are. Be smart, try to have company wherever you go. Avoid the subway. Change your schedule daily. Be alert! Especially when you or your family visits your father. We know he is being kept alive on a ventilator following surgery, and we are posting twenty-four hour armed guards. I suggest you keep in touch with hospital personnel via phone - visiting at this juncture is pointless - for your protection."

"I'd hate for my mother to have this worry on top of what she's already had to deal with."

"Bring her on board, a-sap. She could be a target. In fact, she could be even more vulnerable because the terrorists might believe that your father shared information with her. They might know our laws regarding spousal confidentiality."

"Will I see you again? Have you replaced McMahon?"

"Yes. You may also meet with Detective Grayson from NYPD. We're working closely together. We will be watching, but must count on you to be careful and alert."

I was hired as a temp by a real estate firm. The job was more temporary than I had imagined, and not because I did anything to warrant being let go. The managing partner informed me – after less than two weeks – that their full-time attorney who had been ill would be returning sooner than anticipated. Damn!

Without telling either FBI or NYPD, I followed through with my own plan. Facebook and Twitter were the easiest venues. I had written and rewritten my postings twenty times before going public.

"This message is for the men who targeted my father, Sam Marcus, and managed to get into the courtroom to murder him. We have been told that you fear our family's retribution. Well, guess what? Our father told us nothing about you guys, though all the Marcus adults have their suspicions. iIt couldn't be the Mafia, given dad's focus exclusively on procuring illegal equipment for Middle Eastern countries. The Mafia doesn't give a damn about that part of the world. So, let's guess. Could it be the Taliban? ISIS? Hezbollah? The Muslim Brotherhood? Anyone of these terrorist organizations might be involved.

"Sam Marcus, near death after his assault, never told us what he brought in, which countries, beyond Israel, he helped. The prosecution posed some hypotheses, but never solidly proved the where. They found the money, which they appropriated.

"FBI is looking for your inside assistant. They will find him. And he knows what we don't. Since we despise that unknown individual, I suggest your turn your murderous intent in his direction. We wish you success there.

"You may not believe these messages from a family member. I can almost appreciate your suspicion, since your group has no doubt been the target for assasination, wherever and whoever you are. Please believe we do not have the information and resources to hurt you. But the FBI and your home country do."

I received many hundreds of responses to these posts. Adiga was furious with me. So was Larry, who decided that I lost my mind. Carlos, more circumspect, suggested that I stay with him in San Francisco. My college friends, Stanford study group mates, even my hairdresser, all worried about me. Strangely enough, I felt lighter.

Only Aunt Lily supported me: "Fuck those bastards! Being proactive rather than hiding in a corner sucking our thumbs, that's the way to go. You are our leader." She offered me her guest bedroom, but I refused, reluctant to put her into potential danger. And, assuring me that my nasty response to her son Brett was understandable, she forgave me.

It's not accurate that only Aunt Lily supported me. Elisa, though under so much stress herself, asked how she could help.

I needed to talk to someone who wouldn't lecture me, or to tell me to relocate, find a job, etc. Dr. Held would fit the bill. So I called him, and flew to Chicago for some sessions, mom paying.

We got off to a bad start, my doing. He was too jazzy for my taste.

"Maybe you shrinks, with your so-called magic, never really help anyone. Who can cure chronic distrust? Your patients feel warm and fuzzy here with you, then have to go into the bleak, nasty world. And let's not forget you are well paid. So can you be trusted? Maybe you go home and beat your wife and kids, and have illicit sex."

"Hostility wall up for protection, Sally? It's like when we first met. Why the need for so much distance?"

"Sorry. Even to my own ears, I sound vicious." Tears poured down my cheeks as I struggled for air; head down, arms circling myself, choking on my next words: "I need help. I hate needing anyone's help."

Handing me a box of tissues, he half-whispered, "Yes." He waited for me to compose myself, adding, "Facing that is the beginning of wisdom."

Jonah could not have guessed that I had been staying in Chicago. When I called him, I heard predictable wariness in his voice.

"Well, Sally, this is a surprise. I hadn't wanted to bother you by calling again, to ask how you and your mom are doing."

"You sound so formal, Jonah."

"What would you expect?" Said sharply, he shifted to a softer delivery: "I'm not unhappy to hear from you. But why, after so long?"

At his suggestion, we met in a remote sculpture gallery in the Chicago Art Museum on a cool, sunny late October morning. He looked beautiful to me, very like when we first had found each other. But in response to my hug, he stiffened.

"I've managed to infect you with my distrust. Who could blame you after what I put you through?"

Over the next two hours, we walked and we talked, we noshed and we talked. We both said, "I love you." Until our more authentic message, 'we're saying goodbye again' was spoken, we were marking time. Jonah, comme d'habitude, was the more courageous, putting that into words: "We both need to move on. Too much hurt and misunderstanding has created distrust that is unlikely to ever lift."

I expressed my own sadness and gratitude, as we hugged and kissed at the exit, unshed tears filming my vision as I watched Jonah walk away.

I called Carlos from the airport, needing to connect with someone who cares. Though his secretary said her boss was in a staff meeting, she did put me through, sounding annoyed. With me? With Carlos taking my call? Jealous? Who knew? Who gives a damn?

After asking how I was - sad, with a blown ego - Carlos asked if he could call me tonight. "Please fly out, darlin' - check Friday's schedule. I miss you. I'll be waiting."

Carlos never mentioned my father on that call, or in any way made reference to his own frightening experience. He did inquire as to mom, referring to her as "your madre." I wanted to ask him, if, as a criminal defense attorney, had he ever been in a dangerous situation during a contentious trial. I never did ask.

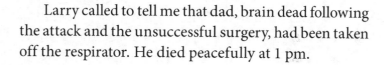

Larry called to tell me that dad, brain dead following the attack and the unsuccessful surgery, had been taken off the respirator. He died peacefully at 1 pm.

CHAPTER 26

ays after my return to New York, on exiting my elevator I discovered Khaled Adiga leaning against the wall next to my apartment, writing.

"Now what?" This time I couldn't conceal a smile.

"I have a present for you," he joked, his laughter extending to those dark eyes.

"Oh yeah?" I keyed us into my place, feeling some pleasure in flirting. We're both safe; he's married, his wedding ring prominent.

Once seated, Khaled proved true to his word: "We have identified the man who helped our killer. Julio Diaz, a 31 year old clerk in the courthouse, a legal resident with no priors. Want to hear more?"

"Damn it, of course!"

"Mr. Diaz, a Dominican, lives with his wife and two young children, as well as with his wife's brother, in Washington Heights near the GW Bridge. He's here since high school, has led an exemplary life. So how and why did he connect up with the assassin? The two men met in Julio's neighborhood, in a small beer joint. The Egyptian initiated conversation. Julio told this guy he was in a panic over money since his wife quit her job before their second baby was born the previous May. The killer had him."

"Do you know that bastard's real name? Did this Julio tell you much about him?"

"Diaz had a name and a cell phone number for the shooter, who called himself Abul Zabari. The guy had flown into Toronto from London. We don't know how he traveled to New York. He had a passport in that name, likely an excellent fake. Zabari and Diaz hung out together during early July. We believe that Zabari had originally followed Diaz home from the courthouse to prepare the way for their so-called 'accidental' meeting. He offered Diaz what must have seemed like a fortune: $10,000 in cash. Diaz grabbed it. He told us he was desperate to move to a bigger apartment, that his landlord was threatening to put them out in the street since his wife's brother moved in, and they now have two children, all in a tiny one-bedroom."

"What was Diaz told he had to do for the money?"

"He had to let Zabari in the side door of the courthouse on several occasions. Only guards escorting prisoners to court are permitted to use that entrance. Diaz admitted being suspicious as to the man's motive, but was reassured that Zabari was an observer for some friends who might be unfairly implicated during the trial. On the day of the shooting, since he needed Diaz' help smuggling the gun into the courthouse, Zabari added that he planned to scare Marcus into silence, not hurt him. Diaz was horrified at the thought of being an accomplice, admitted to not believing Zabari, but feared for his life if he failed to cooperate. The poor schmuck knows that he faces a long prison term. In fact, his willingness to plead guilty to conspiracy to commit multiple murders is his only chance to not die in prison an old man. He also knows he could be a target of the killer's colleagues."

"What does he know about them?"

"Diaz claims not to know anything more than what he told us. He was too scared to ask, and Zabari was too sophisticated to have shared anything of value. Though Diaz contributed to a terrible crime, the funny thing is, he's quite naïve. I'm inclined to believe that he hadn't guessed when he first agreed to help Zabari the extent of what that man was planning."

"Khaled, is the family safe now? You know what I did – the interviews on the morning shows, Facebook, Twitter. You were furious with me. I've heard from thousands by now – all supportive. No threats. But I'm still scared, for myself, for my mother, my brother's family. Dad is still on life support, unlikely to survive. Does your arresting Diaz mean that it's all over?"

"Whoever paid Zabari may feel they did not get their money's worth because your father could survive. He'll never return to the states, and in fact, his handlers may kill him. Live your life. We're confident no one has any reason as this juncture to go after you or your family."

"Then I guess I should say thank you."

"That would be nice. We wanted to make it right, notwithstanding we cannot undo what has been done."

Khaled shook my hand, and with his warm smile

announced his leaving: "Anything else you need, any questions, just call."

"One last question. Where are you from?"

"New Jersey. Fort Lee. Born and raised there. Still a Jersey boy."

Telephone calls to mom and Elisa seemed to help them. Elisa said she and Larry have decided to keep their children in private school. My mother, who had been advised that dad would be transferred to a long-term facility in New Jersey, specialists in brain injured victims, was actually relieved at his death. She is still very sad, but not depressed, and accepts that visiting an unconscious, unresponsive Sam Marcus did no good for him, and was devastating for her. That's over.

CHAPTER 27

I flew into San Francisco two days in advance of a conference on separation of powers, anticipating seeing some of my Stanford pals before the formality of the weekend. Carlos, when told of my plans, ordered me –"Bring your passport; we'll fly over to Baja.

As I exited JetBlue baggage claim with two bulging suitcases, there was Carlos, grinning, "Well, Sal, darlin', this is to make up for my not collecting you the last time around!" He gave me a quick kiss, while grabbing the heavier of the suitcases, leading us to his Land Rover. His smirk when I mentioned staying at an airbnb assured me he would have made a different choice. But then again, he's not broke.

Heading east into wine country, whistling, singing Spanish folk songs, Carlos effectively avoided my questions. Exhausted, I napped. Two hours later, after a quick stop for gas and a snack, he pulled into a sprawling pink and green hacienda-like bed and breakfast.

"Carlos, what is this? I have to be at the university tomorrow night – why are we here?"

"Don't kvech, baby, just enjoy. Look at this…" He pointed to acres of shocking green fields meeting an azure sky. He had registered us as Mr. & Mrs. before tipping the bellboy to bring the suitcases to our room.

"Come on, Sally, relax, you're in for a treat." We

trekked ¼-mile to the wine shop where we got to sample their latest cabernets and chardonnays while conversing with the shop's gracious young hostess. Then, tipsy and hungry, we returned to our room, where as planned in advance by my 'director,' we were served a delicious dinner of marinated shrimp, rice and plantains. With more of that delicious wine.

"Talk to me, Sally. Tell me what I'm waiting to hear."

We were nude, having made love on the narrow, pillow-topped bed, sun streaming in through the large uncovered window, overlooking a distant pool. Unsure of how to respond, but not of my feelings, I begged Carlos, "No talking now, maybe soon." I wasn't certain of what he expected, but did know that I was nowhere ready for any relationship-changing conversation.

Carlos dropped me off at Stanford twenty-four hours later, with two comments: "Hope you feel as good as I do, cara mia." And, "I'll pick you up after the conference on Sunday." No question as to whether I wanted this – which I did – so I cracked, "Bossy as ever, aren't you?" My grin and lingering kiss contradicted these words.

Our reunion was similar to Barnard's, but different. It was alike in that the competition ran high: who's married, has a child, is more in shape, has begun a great career. Well, I was fine with the 'in shape' part, but struck out otherwise. Meeting my former study mates, viewing photos of spouses and babies, I briefly regretted coming. The old wall grew as several shared impressive career moves, some in firms I had read about in the Wall Street Journal. Then, Leslie made a joke, Bruce gave me a warm and too strong bear hug, even Amy – could she have softened? – told me how much she missed me, how our relationship had meant a great deal to her. I volunteered that she had been on target years ago about Jonah and me jumping into a relationship. Nodding, she said: "You're a healthier version of yourself."

With Stanford friends, the family's sordid tale would not prove as enveloping as in New York, where it seemed everyone knew the Marcus' story. These friends had known some details, several had even called me during the trial and after dad's assault, and his publicized death. Almost everyone from my old study group expressed concern for me and for my family, then let it go. We embraced fun, dancing to rock, eating and drinking, showing off with strenuous running and wrestling games. Of course, there were the excellent lectures and workshops from legal stars, encouraging us to civic and political engagement. Just before Carlos picked me up, I was introduced to a law school employment counselor who invited me to call her the following week. That date went onto my phone's calendar.

Carlos refused to say where we were headed, but once the taxi driver passed his exit, it became clear that we were going to the airport. Just prior to security, Carlos handed me my boarding pass: Mexico City. I'd never been there, could have used some down time but I was not unhappy. Nevertheless, I did complain: "How am I supposed to take your always doing your own thing – not asking me. Had you asked, I would have signed on." His "Okay, Sal," accompanied by a shrug and a smile, was a contradiction; his collaborating gene is underpowered.

We spent Tuesday and Wednesday racing around this multifaceted, teeming city, with me slightly altitude-sick but struggling to fake it. Carlos was my enthusiastic, all-knowing tour guide, leading us to the Museum of Anthropology, the Zoo, and to parks and shops reminiscent of Madison Avenue, where he bought me a stunning silver bracelet. That evening we attended the Ballet Folklorico followed by a late, late dinner at el Mundo Grande. I was wiped out, while Carlos was just fine.

"Pack up, Sal. We're outa here early tomorrow morning – right after breakfast."

"No, Carlos. I want to sleep in. I was exhausted after the conference; now I'm dead. Why do we have to leave so early?"

"You sound like my five year-old nephew. We have to."

The following morning, he awakened me with an unromantic: "Get your body in the shower. I'll pack. Then breakfast and we hit the road."

"Where to?"

"You'll see." To that, I snickered, "Not again," but obeyed his instructions without further complaint.

This glorious morning saw us in a rented Mustang convertible with Carlos focused on negotiating the modern, winding mountain road. About fifty miles into the trip, he pointed to the road sign: Cuernavaca, and soon exited. Of course, I knew that his parents lived here, and was certain his plan included my meeting them.

"Oh, I've always wanted to see this town, and of course, to meet your parents. My old roommate at Barnard studied Spanish here – she raved about the gardens."

An audible grunt, but silence from this normally chatty guy. Within minutes, he parked in front of a modest white and turquoise stucco ranch house, graced by flowers of every size and color. To my inquiry, "Do you know the names of these flowers?," Carlos responded, "There's a lady inside who has all those answers."

"Bienvenido, Sally. We are delighted to finally meet you. Calls from Carlos, he says, 'someday you'll meet Sally.' But it never happened 'til now." With that, his mom led us into an immaculate, stark white kitchen. His dad jumped off a stool to shake my hand, while Carlos' younger sister, Sophia, hugged and kissed me. The family represents a rainbow of colors - mom white, dad and Sophia darker than cocoa-hued Carlos. My guy seemed on edge, insisting that I join him on the small backyard patio. His mother protested – it's so hot at this hour – but as usual, his vote was the deciding one. He touched his mother's cheek tenderly: "Mom, we'll only be outside for a few minutes. Then you can stuff us all you like!"

I was led through the glass patio door to the edge of the small cement patio. Truthfully, I wasn't all that shocked when Carlos got down on one knee, and in Spanish and English, asked me to marry him. Sweating profusely in the stifling heat, shaking with nervousness, words deserted me. Carlos, holding a stunning diamond ring, reached for my left hand, before finally responding to my silence.

"Sally – what's happening? You must have known I want to marry you. That I would propose. You seem upset. Please, say something."

I shook my head. "I love you, Carlos, never doubt that. But I am nowhere ready to be married. It's as if what went on in my family, not only my father's disappearance and murder, but my whole childhood - so different from yours - and I don't only mean culturally - all of it - stopped me from growing up. I'm emotionally an adolescent. I've never supported myself, lived alone, even begun to have a career. How can I make grown-up choices, like getting married, when I'm sure I've made so many of the wrong ones up to now? And you are so confident, so willing to make decisions for me. I see myself tempted to be compliant again. But I know - I'm certain - I must focus on developing my own solid self. And, Carlos, how would you eventually feel if I never became a full partner?" Here I smiled, adding to relieve the stress, "You love that now, but one day… Our relationship can only benefit from both of us as equals, and for that, I need time."

Carlos, out of character, remained silent, watching and listening. Had I crushed his spirit? He needed me, I thought, when most times I need him. Reaching for his hand, raising it to my lips, I pleaded, "Please give us some time, darling. And hold onto that gorgeous ring!"

I watched him struggle to regain composure, to find his words. It had occurred to me earlier that his family might have known of his plan, and be waiting to celebrate with us. "Please assure them that we love each other, but we need more time before moving to the next step. Could you do that for us? Or are you too hurt, too angry to trust me?" I finally shut up, waiting anxiously for his response. It was perfect: "You're worth waiting for, cara mia." Arms around each other, we entered the kitchen together, into the enveloping arms of his madre.

My cell phone rang. It was Larry. Mom decided with the family to sit a delayed shiver after all. The news silenced me. I didn't want to leave here. Larry concurred. "Stay. We'll deal with arrangements. Mom agrees. You did enough."

"And Larry, you were right. Remember telling me at graduation that I should take the California Bar exam? Well, I am planning to do exactly that after a refresher course on campus.

"Right now I'm with Carlos and his family. They feel like family."

"Okay, kid, but…"

I interrupted him. "Don't worry. I am not rushing into anything. Love you all. Bye."